Rave Reviews for Chris' *Night of the Living* the Stage Play

"The dialogue is snappy and the acting is intense… with excellent make-up effects. Music is used effectively to create suspense and tension especially when it's instrumental and ambient. The overall effect is visually striking and frightening. There's no reason Cook's *Night of the Living Dead* shouldn't have standing room only for the rest of its run!"

- August Krickel
Free Times
Columbia, SC

"An evening full of scary surprises for the audience. Those who come to the show will be in for a night of cannibalistic ghouls, gunshots, fire effects, and a final bloodbath!"

- Julia Rogers Hook
The Columbia Star
Columbia, SC

"Adapted by Christofer Cook, the play features Hollywood-level special FX make-up, stage combat, firearms, and hordes of man-eating zombies! A true classic of American cinema is now the hottest theatrical event in Columbia of 2013! It promises to shock, thrill, chill, and excite audiences currently on a steady diet of *The Walking Dead*. Yes, they're coming to get you, Columbia!"

- Gus Hart
Jasper Magazine
Columbia, SC

Rave Reviews for Christofer Cook's
Dracula of Transylvania
with Script Advisement by
Dacre Stoker

"Dracula lives! Lugosi was the first to take it to the stage. 90 years later, the new [Christofer Cook and Dacre Stoker's] *Dracula of Transylvania* adaptation runs on stage through October. The big night will be on Halloween in West Columbia at the High Voltage Theatre!"

- Aaron Sagers,
Travel Channel
New York, NY

"When it comes to theatre, Cook isn't afraid to stare into the abyss, adapting and producing works of horror for the stage… It is as much a celebration of Bram Stoker's life as it is [a celebration of] the novel."

- Alison Lang
Rue Morgue Magazine
Toronto, Canada

"*Dracula of Transylvania* is about as close to Bram Stoker as you can probably get. His literary DNA is all over this play!"

- Tyler Ryan
ABC / WOLO-TV
Columbia, SC

"A wonderful mixture of suspense, romance, subtle humor, and well,… let's not forget the blood."

- Angie Holland
The Oskaloosa Herald
Mahaska County, Iowa

"High Voltage Scores with new Dracula! Christofer Cook and Dacre Stoker, great-grand-nephew of Bram, have infused fresh life into a 19th-century classic; in doing so, they have created a viable stage *Dracula* for the new millennium, remaining true to the source novel while exploring unique dramatic territory suggested by live (or undead) performance."

- Meredith Merridew
The Free Times
Columbia, SC

"The definitive version for live theatre!
Certain to become a 'modern-day classic'
and a masterpiece for the ages."

- Miles Richards
The Columbia Star
Columbia, SC

"Bram Stoker's 1897 plot is followed closely. In fact, Christofer Cook and Dacre Stoker are successful in three major areas; Flowing language, expanded characterizations, and visual moments of eerie silence on stage… the effect is genuinely chilling."

- Gus Hart
Jasper Magazine
Columbia, SC

"Like any self-respecting vampire,
Cook draws fresh blood from time-honored tropes
and breathes into them, new life!"

- Dacre Stoker, Co-Author
Dracul and *Dracula, the Undead*

"…a *Dracula* that offers a satisfying live alternative to decades of cinematic gore and computer-generated mayhem. The adaptors' respect for the source material retains Bram Stoker's florid, near-Shakespearean prose without sacrificing suspense, thrills, chills, or good old-fashioned action. This is the purest of portraits…"

- August Krickel
OnStage Columbia

"*Dracula of Transylvania* comes to the stage for your Halloween enjoyment. It's October! The best month for a horror show!"

- Luke Gonzales
Escalon Times,
Oakdale, California

"*Dracula of Transylvania* is no drawing room mystery a la Agatha Christie. It pulls from Bram Stoker's original novel all the gothic romance, the terror, the magic, and dark atmosphere inherent in the original story. From the polite cobblestone streets of Victorian London to the wilds of the dangerous Carpathians in Romania!"

- Joshua Morriston
Turlock Journal
Turlock, California

"It's that time of the year for thrills and chills at the Denair Gaslight Theater with Christofer Cook's *Dracula of Transylvania*."

-Editor
Denair Pulse
Denair, California

Published Plays / Books by the Author

Amityville 1925

Dracula of Transylvania

Phantom of the Opera

The Legend of Sleepy Hollow

A Christmas Carolinian

Hallow Evil

AMITYVILLE 1925

A Play of Horror
in Two Acts

CHRISTOFER COOK

authorHOUSE®

AuthorHouse™
1663 Liberty Drive
Bloomington, IN 47403
www.authorhouse.com
Phone: 833-262-8899

© 2022 Christofer Cook. All rights reserved.

No part of this book may be reproduced, stored in a retrieval system, or transmitted by any means without the written permission of the author.

Published by AuthorHouse 08/31/2022

ISBN: 978-1-6655-6920-0 (sc)
ISBN: 978-1-6655-6919-4 (e)

Library of Congress Control Number: 2022915835

Print information available on the last page.

Any people depicted in stock imagery provided by Getty Images are models, and such images are being used for illustrative purposes only.
Certain stock imagery © Getty Images.

This book is printed on acid-free paper.

Because of the dynamic nature of the Internet, any web addresses or links contained in this book may have changed since publication and may no longer be valid. The views expressed in this work are solely those of the author and do not necessarily reflect the views of the publisher, and the publisher hereby disclaims any responsibility for them.

Caution

Professionals and amateurs are hereby warned that *AMITYVILLE 1925*, A Play of Horror in Two Acts, by Christofer Cook is subject to a royalty. It is fully protected under the copyright laws of the United States of America, and of all countries covered by the International Copyright Union (Including the Dominion of Canada and the rest of the British Commonwealth), and of all countries covered by the Pan-American Copyright Convention and the Universal Copyright Convention, and all countries with which the United States has reciprocal copyright relations. All rights, including professional, amateur, motion picture, recitation, lecturing, public reading, radio broadcasting, television, video or sound recording, all other forms of mechanical or electronic reproduction, such as information storage, retrieval systems and photocopying, downloading, streaming video, social media channels, and the rights of translation into foreign languages are strictly reserved. Particular emphasis is laid upon the question of readings, permission and terms for which must be secured from the author in writing.

The stage performance rights for *AMITYVILLE 1925*, A Play of Horror in Two Acts, by Christofer Cook are controlled exclusively by the playwright. No professional or non-professional performance of the play may be given without obtaining in advance the written permission of the dramatist and paying the requisite royalty fees. All inquiries concerning rights to the play should be addressed to;

Christofer Cook
ChristoferCook64@gmail.com
(803) 429-8839
149 Oakpointe Drive
Lexington, SC 29072

Special Note

Anyone receiving permission to produce *AMITYVILLE 1925*, a Play of Horror in Two Acts, by Christofer Cook, is subject to the following proviso; Producing theatres, schools, and any and all other community groups, are required to give due authorship credit to the playwright as the sole and exclusive author of the play. The by-line should read as follows (and either listing is appropriate); *Amityville 1925* by Christofer Cook, OR Christofer Cook's *Amityville 1925*. Either one of these two creditings must appear on all posters, websites, social-media advertising, programs, flyers, postcards, T-shirts and any and all other promotional printing in connection with productions of the play and/or a production thereof. The name of the playwright must appear on a separate line, in which no other name appears, immediately beneath the title (or above the title) and in size of type equal to 50% of the largest letter used for the title of the play. No person, firm, nor entity may receive credit larger than that accorded the playwright. Failure to comply with this proviso may result in a delay of the production's opening and/or the company's accruing the necessary costs of re-printing the promotional materials in question.

A Note on Music

AMITYVILLE 1925 was written in collaboration with musical composer Brandon Vaughn of 'Raven Chronicles'. The premiere production employed the talents of Mr. Vaughn and 'Raven Chronicles' to create pieces of music and sounds to bridge transitions between major scenes as well as to underscore certain moments within the play.

Now available on Digital Download (CD by Special Request), Mr. Vaughn's exquisite composition is available for free licensing upon payment of royalties for the play. Should you choose to use his original music for your production of *AMITYVILLE 1925,* a free digital download sample can be requested at;

Chaoticfractal@icloud.com
(512) 887-0752
www.RavenChronicles.net

Columbia Playwright Rises Again with New Horror Production

Preview by Gus Hart
The Free Times
October 19th, 2021

Much like the vampires and creatures that fueled his imagination as a child, Christofer Cook has risen from a self-imposed hibernation to terrify the Midlands once again.

A theatrical quadruple-threat who acts, write, directs, and produces, Cook staged lavish, outdoor adaptation of classic thrillers under the banner of his High Voltage Theatre Company from 2002 to 2013. These included "Frankenstein" staged at the Granby Locks Outdoor Performance Space in Cayce, "Dracula of Transylvania", "Phantom of the Opera", and seven iterations of "The Legend of Sleepy Hollow" staged at West Columbia's Riverwalk Amphitheater. The latter complete with a live horse, a headless horseman, and plenty of stage magic and practical special effects.

Now, Cook is back with Theatre Mysterium, a rebranding of High Voltage, which debuts his original work "Amityville 1925" just in time for Halloween at the Columbia Music Festival's ArtSpace. The playwright explained that the new name more accurately reflects what High Voltage had evolved into: a production company specializing in suspense, mystery, and the macabre. "Amityville 1925" developed from Cook's lifelong fascination with the horror genre and aptly fits into this new ethos.

A 1977 book by Jay Anson, "The Amityville Horror", chronicles the misadventure of the real-life Lutz family, residents who claimed to have been driven out of the house by supernatural happenings; it quickly became a best-seller, inspiring a film starring James Brolin and Marot Kidder, with multiple sequels and adaptations. And Cook, after years of research into the infamous house at 112 Ocean Avenue (now 108 Ocean Avenue) in Long Island's Amityville village, has been enticed by the tale. It influenced him to work on his prequel "Amityville 1925" and a similar-styled house's picture centers on promotional material prominently.

Cook was quick to stress, however, that his work is a completely original prequel which speculates on what may have befallen the home's original owners in the 1920's. Therefore, "there are no oozing walls, and no fly infestations," hallmark occurrences in both the novel and the 1979 film. The resulting script is "a few parts Hitchcock, and a few parts Agatha Christie," with thrills and chills galore, he said.

While revealing no secrets, the director promised plenty of "poltergeist-like activity" such as ghostly apparitions, furniture and other household items sent careening across stage by unseen hands, and a lightning and thunder show. Cook went so far as to require each cast member to sign a non-disclosure agreement relating to the delivery of certain special effects, both from an earnest desire to preserve secrecy for maximum shock value, and as a nod to B-movie impresarios of yore, such as William Castle and Roger Corman who concocted similar publicity stratagems.

The cast includes Frank Thompson, Zsuzsa Manna, Charlie Goodrich, Katie Mixon, Stephanie Walker, James Nolan, Landry Phillips, and Charlie Grace Douglas. Cook stressed Cook that the spookiness notwithstanding, his play also focuses on the characters' humanity. "We've got a family in crisis, trying to live a life as happily as they can."

The path to Amityville has been a long one, coming more than eight years since he last helmed a cast in a stage production. A Columbia native, Cook earned a Master of Fine Arts degree in Directing from Chicago's Roosevelt University, and then spent a decade acting and directing with a number of professional companies around the country. He returned to Columbia in the early 2000's and it led to a career shift into academia, with teaching gigs in Drama and Acting at Newberry, Limestone, and Midlands Technical Colleges.

His hit "The Legend of Sleepy Hollow" evolved from a script prepared for his students at Tech to perform, Cook, remembered. The group later took on the name "High Voltage" from a rusted warning sign leading to a power grid at the Beltline campus's theater. "We felt it represented the sort of raw, 'in your face' style of show I had done in Chicago", Cook explained.

Subsequent shows included a stage adaptation of "Reservoir Dogs" which featured aggressive acting, readlistc stage violence, and plentiful stage blood. His transition to horror was natural, especially when local audiences began filling seats to maximum capacity at annual Halloween productions. 2013 arguabley marked High Voltage's creative pinnacle, beginning with the premiere of Cook's original adaptation of "Night of the Living Dead" and, after, Cook's original "Dracula of Transylvania" (a collaboration with Dacre Stoker, great-grand nephew of Bram) once again staged at the river.

But, while popularity soared, support from local funding sources dried up, and Cook put High Voltage on hiatus in 2014.

He became something of a journeyman on the city's art scene in the years after. He played title roles in local Shakespeare productions; was a guest artist at Trustus and USC, and worked as Santa Claus amid the pandemic, a role he's set to reprise this holiday season. Still, Cook sees his future in writing, in part fueled by this "Sleepy Hollow" work, which has been performed by at least twenty regional companies across the country. This is part of a career strategy, so that my works can have an incubation lab of sorts, get polished, then submitted to major regional and community theatres across the US", he revealed.

The author conceded the challenges faced in staging one's own work. Scheduling and logistical conflicts have plagued his rehearsal process, but the company has persisted. While Tatway Tattoos of Lexington is the title sponsor along with partial support from Leading-Up of Columbia,

Cook and his wife Carolina fund the bulk of their work. "Every time we produce we forget how expensive it is to do even the simplest of shows. But we commit."

"Amityville 1925"
Dates; Oct, 21 – Oct 31
General Admission; $20
Columbia Music Festival Association
The ArtSpace at 914 Pulaski Street,
Columbia, South Carolina
Reservations; **TicketLeap.com**

Amityville 1925,
Seven Years in the Making for Christofer Cook

Review by Cindi Boiter
The Jasper Project
October 23rd, 2021

Seven years in the making, playwright and founder of Theatre Mysterium, Christofer Cook, brings his new play **"Amityville 1925"** to the black box performance space at Columbia Music Festival Association, 914 Pulaski Street in Columbia's Vista. Inspired by mythology surrounding the famed house at the center of "The Amityville Horror" franchise, Cook's cast enacts a tale about the Moynahan family, a real family who occupied the home in 1925. In Cook's imagination, the Irish Catholic family of five is transplanted to Amityville, NY taking up residence at 112 Ocean Avenue, the same house that has appeared to be malevolently sneering down at us in all our scary movie-induced nightmares since the first film debuted in 1979.

In Cook's play, the family arrives at their new home with their furnishings intact due to the kindness of Jesse Purdy, the patriarch John Moynahan's best friend. They immediately have the home blessed in traditional Catholic fashion by the local priest Father Fitzgerald but, despite the ostensible blessings bestowed by the man of the cloth, something is awry from the start. Noises from beneath the floorboards, pops and snaps from the fireplace, toppled furniture and books flying through the air. Everything one would expect from a home we hope to be haunted. But the Moynahan family of three adult children and parents are smarter than the average haunted household-dwellers and they use their deductive powers and Irish intellects to solve the mystery of a house that has a mind of its own.

Or do they?

"**Amityville 1925**" is a world premiere play with exceedingly strong bones and quite a bit of meat on them, to boot. Having seen the first ever public performance of the play on its opening night of Thursday, October 21, I was engaged by where the story was going, where it took me, and impressed by the scenery along the way.

Cook has assembled an excellent cast of actors, each holding their own and contributing singularly significant pieces to the puzzle. The cast successfully performs as one expects an ensemble to do with no weak links and no characters overshadowing others.

The fourth wall having been delightfully broken from the onset as the players approach the stage via the audience, pausing on the steps of the home to acknowledge the beginning of their occupancy of the house, as well as the beginning of the play, various characters return to their conversation with the audience throughout the performance. The convention works well as a comfortable narrative device with little to no meta-referential disruption.

As family matriarch Catherine Moynahan, Zsuzsa Manna neatly walks a narrow path of being both devoutly religious but still intellectually astute and perceptive. Her Irish accent was captivating as was that of her on-stage spouse, Frank Thompson in the role of John Moynahan.

The three Moynahan siblings, Stephanie Walker as Eileen, Katie Mixon as Marguerite, and James Nolan as Thomas, are strongly portrayed. Walker's performance was particularly engaging, evoking comparison with that of Samantha Sloyan's Bev Keane on the Netflix drama *Midnight Mass*. Even on opening night the audience got a sense of the essence of the sibling's unique personalities which, as the run progresses, I feel certain will acquire even more depth. James Nolan's performance suggested a far more mature actor than I expected when I recognized his youth. As he more fully actualizes his role I would expect to see more of the youthful anger and frustration the character Thomas suggests as the play goes on.

The most challenging role of the play was that of Father Fitzgerald which Charlie Goodrich accomplished with ease. Goodrich fully possessed the variation required of his role, leading the audience to believe that Father Fitzgerald was quite the actor himself.

The fact that this playwright/production team put a performance of this caliber together is an unusual and quite remarkable accomplishment and they deserve high praise. The play is grounded, smart, wryly funny in unexpected places, (here's to soda bread and rotting corpses), and thoroughly entertaining. It may, in fact, be the best thing you'll see this Halloween season.

The next time I see it, and I really want to see it again, I hope it will be at a more professional and more hospitable venue (other than the Columbia Music Festival Association's ArtSpace) with a larger crew, a bigger budget, - though Theatre Mysterium clearly did a lot with a little – and all the whistles and bells a well-conceived and soundly performed piece of theatre art like **"Amityville 1925"** deserves.

"Amityville 1925"
Dates; Oct, 21 – Oct 31
General Admission; $20
Columbia Music Festival Association
The ArtSpace at 914 Pulaski Street,
Columbia, South Carolina
Reservations; **TicketLeap.com**

In *Amityville 1925*, a Veteran Cast Lifts Local Playwright's Chilling Prequel

Review by August Krickel
Post and Courier
October 28th, 2021

There is no equivocation and no punches are pulled in playwright Christofer Cook's new work, 'Amityville 1925', presented by his new, rebranded Theatre Mysterium. The creepy house at 112 Ocean Avenue in Long Island's Amityville community is definitely haunted. Yet there are far more complex factors at work in Cook's original stage prequel to the events depicted in the 1977 book 'The Amityville Horror' and its 1979 film adaptation. With an A-list of Columbia acting talent and the eloquence of the author's flowing prose, all components ultimately combined for a satisfying couple of hours of seasonal Halloween thrills.

At an opening weekend matinee on October 17th, Frank Thompson led the ensemble cast as the patriarch of the Moynahan family, sturdy Irish immigrants who have achieved a modest level of upper middle class success, and who have moved into a new home built for them by kindly Mr. Purdy (Landry Phillips). Thompson somehow seemed the most authentically Celtic of the actors, embracing ancestral superstitions from the old country as he confronted unseen and malevolent forces.

Zsuzsa Manna, Katie Mixon, Stephanie Walker, and James Nolan portrayed the mother, elder sister, younger sister, and teen son of the family, respectively, with Charlie Goodrich as a young priest, and Charlie Grace Douglas as a significant Amityville resident. All were believable in their portrayals, with Nolan seemingly growing into manhood before our eyes as he too stepped up to defend his family. A comely Irish lass or two flirting with and/or attempting to seduce a vulnerable young priest is always a reliable and entertaining trope, and the possibility of spectral influence or possession gave added material into which the actors readily dove.

The audience was treated to a detailed and realistic set, courtesy of scenic designer West Jenkins. Set decoration including a period record player, telephone and chaise lounge helped to establish the 1925 setting, as did costumes by Lydia Latham, and a structure suggesting a front porch covered with vividly colorful fall foliage was particularly effective. An important upstairs bedroom setting was located to the rear of the set, and the audience's imagination took care of supplying the stairs and doors that would have led there. And yes, the ominous quarter moon upstairs windows were present – just as they are in almost every Dutch Colonial Revival home from that era. A brooding original score by Brandon Vaughn helped to complete the overall atmosphere of gloom and impending doom.

Much of the play's appeal was dependent on unexpected plot twists and turns, so it's hard to reveal much. Suffice to say that the anticipated poltergeist effects transpired as a result of dark and deadly deeds from an earlier century. Several characters were revealed to be sleepwalkers, making them somehow more susceptible to arcane influences, and one character had a major secret that set many of the plot developments into motion.

There were absolutely moments of genuine suspense, mainly in the classic Hitchcock vein of waiting for an expected fright, rather than the fright itself. Unfortunately a number of supernatural occurrences were underserved by the limitation of the production budget. One accepted why the characters were terrified, but that terror usually remained on the stage only.

The roots of the evil that plagued the house would have been sufficient for a satisfying ghost story, but much of the play's action involved a murder mystery. Much like the ending of a film by M. Night Shyamalan, an unforeseeable twist brought these disparate storylines together where a least likely suspect is revealed as the mastermind behind it all. This all-American family had the fortitude and ingenuity to resist and prevail.

The lilt in the actor's delivery of the author's dialogue gave a poetic quality to the already articulate script, and passages where characters reflected on life and mortality were moving indeed. Similarly, the skill of the veteran cast easily brought to life this real family from an earlier time. 'Amityville 1925' is admirable at creating a fictional backstory for a well-known horror franchise, and the skill of the author and his cast combined to make for a season-appropriate night of chills and suspense.

"Amityville 1925"
Dates; Oct, 21 – Oct 31
General Admission; $20
Columbia Music Festival Association
The ArtSpace at 914 Pulaski Street,
Columbia, South Carolina
Reservations; **TicketLeap.com**

Pre-Show Recorded Announcement

By Laura Didio

Used exclusively for the Theatre Mysterium production in October of 2021

"Good Evening.

Welcome to tonight's world premiere production of *Amityville 1925* by Christofer Cook and Theatre Mysterium. My name is Laura Didio. You may have seen me on such shows as *Histories Mysteries*, *Shock Docs*, and the documentary film *My Amityville Horror*.

I'm very familiar with the lore of the house at 112 Ocean Avenue. I was the reporter who, back in 1976, first broke and reported on the story exclusively for Channel 5's Ten O' Clock News in New York.

George and Kathy Lutz' story of the haunting and my subsequent investigation were the forerunners for the best-selling book and movie, *The Amityville Horror*. It has since spawned countless publications, films, and now this exciting new stage play.

Before the play begins, I would like to provide you with a few housekeeping items. First, please be considerate and turn off all phones so as not to disrupt the performance, disturb the actors, or your fellow audience members. Remember that flash pictures and the use of recording devices during the performance are strictly prohibited. There will be a brief ten-minute intermission.

Stay safe, continue to wear your face masks, and social distance when possible. And now, prepare for an evening of thrills and chills as you experience my friend Christofer Cook's latest play, *Amityville 1925*.

For Carolina
and Valentina

"Do not stand at my grave and cry –
I am not there… I did not die."
- Irish Proverb

Characters

John Moynahan .... (Late 40's) Irish Catholic Patriarch
Catherine Moynahan .... (Early 40's) Irish Catholic Matriarch
Eileen Moynahan .... (Late 20's) Irish Catholic Eldest Daughter
Marguerite Moynahan .... (Early 20's) Irish Catholic Middle Child
Thomas Moynahan .... (Late Teens) Irish Catholic Youngest Child
Father Fitzgerald .... (30s) Catholic Priest
Jesse Purdy .... (50s) African-American, Long Island
                                              Architect/Carpenter, and Friend
Agatha Ketchum .... A little Ghost Girl

Setting

ACT I
1925, October, Amityville in Long Island, NY

ACT II
Three Days Later

Amityville 1925, by Christofer Cook, made its world premiere on October 21st of 2021 in Columbia, South Carolina. The play was produced by Theatre Mysterium and opened at the Columbia Music Festival Association ArtSpace. The show was sponsored by Tatway Tattoos, Executive Producer was Carolina Rodriguez. Set design was by West Jenkins, lighting design was by Zenaida Broom, sound design was by Ken Broom, costume design was by Lydia Latham, and original music was composed by Brandon Vaughn. Directed by the author, the cast was as follows;

John Moynahan	Frank Thompson
Catherine Moynahan	Zsuzsa Manna
Eileen Moynahan	Stephanie Walker
Marguerite Moynahan	Katie Mixon
Thomas Moynahan	James Nolan
Father Fitzgerald	Charlie Goodrich
Jesse Purdy	Landry Phillips
Agatha Ketchum	Charlie Grace Douglas

Act I

ACT I

Breakdown of Scenes

Prologue 1

Scene 1   "Taking Possession" 3
Scene 2   "Benediction" 12
Scene 3   "Darkness Manifest" 25
Scene 4   "The Inconvenience of Chastity" 31
Scene 5   "Naked Fear" 41
Scene 6   "This House Doesn't Want Us" 45
Scene 7   "The Noose Tightens" 53
Scene 8   "Mortal Coil" 64

The Scene

(*At rise, we see the beautiful, new interior of a Dutch Colonial home. The entire play takes place on this one set. It is in full view, the duration of the play.*
   It is a crisp October day in 1925. Amityville, Long Island in New York. Pre-show music has been dark and mysterious. General warming lights reveal a living room area center. An oriental rug is Down Center upon which is situated a social cluster comprised of a chaise lounge, a setee, a leather wing back chair, and a couple of small side tables where vintage 1920's magazines and folded newspapers are neatly strewn. A curved floor lamp with tasseled shade stands to the side of the wing back. Art Deco statuettes are creatively spaced about upon tables and in recessed wall openings.
   Upon the damask-papered walls are framed prints of Calvin Coolidge, the Empire State Building, magazine covers featuring flappers, and other assorted deco and nouveau paintings. Off Stage Right just downstage of the wingback is a door leading to the kitchen. On the 'return' wall of which is a shelf with vintage foods, tea tins, and cleaning products of the period. Above this shelf is a 1925 wall calendar. In the corner just inside the door are a couple of brooms, and mops.
   A staircase leads up to an upper tier representing the attic bedroom of John and Catherine Moynahan. Most prominently seen are two, large quarter moon windows indicative of the encasements so closely identified with the original house. Throughout pre-show and house opening, audiences are treated to the effect of quiet lightning flashes outside these windows that look out over the outside world like cat's eyes. Stage Right is Thomas's hallway door. Stage Left is the girls'.
NOTE; *The audience should be immersed in appropriate, instrumental, dark and mysterious music and mood lighting from the moment house is open to the first word of the play. There should be no opening / closing of curtains, no scene changes, no shifting of furniture, no interior blackouts between scenes, and no stage hands entering the world of the play. This will facilitate that the narrative is told cleanly, clearly, and relentlessly from start to finish. And that the sacred space, atmosphere, and universe of the play is honored. Likewise, Curtain Call music should continue to play long after the actors have left the stage and the audience is departing the theatre.*

Prologue

(*"Long Island Autumn"* c. Copyright, 2021 by Christofer Cook)

(As house lights dim, new 'Autumnal' gentle music gradually rises. Warm lighting rises upon the area where tree branches canopy the Downstage Left area just in front of the stage steps. Throughout the Prologue, the music plays and backstage electric fans blow upward upon the branches to create a soft breeze effect as the vibrant leaves are gently flitting about their branches. There is also an intermittent falling of leaves in the vicinity throughout the prologue. At a given moment, John, Catherine, Eileen, Marguerite, and Thomas enter from back of the house. Each one is carrying a final armload of boxes, home goods, luggage, and personal effects. The family gathers to create a lovely tableau. They face the audience and deliver the following verse…)

CATHERINE
Spirits abound in this new land.
Breathin', longin', reachin'
With outstretched tendrils
As woodland branches
Summonin' us into their mysterious lair –
Enfoldin' us into their pagan universe –

JOHN
Where the crickle-crackle of hornbeam twig,
A crush of skimble-skamble stuff,
'Neath the shoes of our children, scuff,
And break into brittle brattle.

EILEEN
Winds whip up in cyclonic fervor,
Whirly-gigs of foliage, bright -
Like omens of the dead season.

Autumn stews its medley;
Hick'ry burned and Katsura sweet, unite
Into buttered rum, sugar maple, orange peel.

THOMAS
Leaves like 'tree feathers' fall, hit sunlight to ignite
Into crimson crests and amber syrup,
And darker colors of
Chocolate-painted parchment.

JOHN
But, in one month's time
October's breath will woo't away
In snaky twirls of wind-swept smoke
From chimneys high in ether cold.

MARGUERITE
At present, we embrace the alien land
We are here now,
Within the within.

CATHERINE
A house that is not quite ours –
Yet, here we'll live,
Yet, here we'll die,
And haunt this domicile
in contented perpetuity.
(Music fades out.)

[End of Prologue]

Scene 1

"Taking Possession"

(George Gershwin's "Rhapsody in Blue" of 1924 begins and underscores the following. The family breaks out of tableau.)

ALL
(Excitedly)

Beautiful. / Yay! / Can we go inside now, Da? / Aye, these things are getting' heavy. / Let's go then…

JOHN
Now, how was that for a new house-warmin' ceremony?

(The family responds with unbridled joy.)

ALL
Sounded great! / Nicely done. / Da, let us in. / Now, can we go?/ Come along, Ma.

(Jesse Purdy enters from Exterior Stage Left with a brand-new wooden shingle in one hand and a shiny set of house keys in the other. He has a smile on his face.)

JESSE
Did I just hear the hullabaloo of new homeowners?

(Laughter)

| 3

JOHN
That ya did, my friend! That ya did.

JESSE
For my 'Host with the Most', another set of keys to the kingdom.

JOHN
He's still callin' me the Host. Thank you, good man.

JESSE
And one more gift. It's only fitting that you have the honors, Mr. John Moynahan. 112 Ocean Avenue, Amityville… is yours. Long Island, New York is happy to have you.

CATHERINE
Thank you, Governor Al Smith!

(Laughter)

JESSE
May the year 1925 always bring you the best of memories!

(Purdy hands him a shingle that reads)…

Moynahan
112 Ocean Ave
Amityville, NY

JOHN
Well, would ya look at that.

(John hangs the shingle on a pre-placed hook on a nearby sign post close to the home's exterior door.)

~ AMITYVILLE 1925 ~

I officially declare thee our home!

(Music swells for a moment. Everyone applauds.)

Young ones, Let's all thank our dear friend Mr. Jesse Purdy for not only designing and building the place but helpin' ta load the furniture. And as we've all worked feverishly to get it into some semblance beyond squalor, I hereby welcome everyone to our new home!

(Piano builds as the youth run into the home. The children all take the boxes and other items to the spots indicated by Catherine's pointing. Thomas runs up the stairs to check out the view outside from the quarter moon windows, Eileen runs to the gramophone and organizes a few records. Marguerite runs to the kitchen wall shelf where the calendar is hanging and marks the date with a pencil.)

JESSE
As promised, the incidentals are done. Damask wall-papering, polished hardwood banisters, door jams wiped down, floors waxed…

EILEEN
It's beautiful, Mr. Purdy!

(As each family member carries a different prop to a specific place for the final décor, they each end up center stage for a second to address the audience.)

CATHERINE
The year 1925 is a buzz of activity in the U.S.

THOMAS
Calvin Coolidge is president.

JESSE
Charlie Chaplin's "The Gold Rush" is released.

MARGUERITE
The first issue of "The New Yorker" Magazine is published.

EILEEN
"Tea for Two" by Marion Harris hits number one.

JOHN
At the eleventh Rose Bowl, the Fighting Irish
whoop the bleedin' pants off Stanford.

THOMAS
Harry Houdini opens a new one-man show in New York City.

MARGUERITE
For six years now, women have earned the right to vote.

EILEEN
And don't forget, this is a time of Prohibition.

CATHERINE
So no one ever drinks a drop of whiskey anymore, anywhere, at anytime.

JOHN
Least ways, not in front of the members of the
"Women's Christian Temperance Union".

(John opens a secret compartment hidden in a sewing table and pulls out a bottle and two glasses.)

CATHERINE
Put that away. Do ya know how early it is?

JOHN
It's two o'clock somewhere.

CATHERINE
Then pour me a wee dram. And one for Jesse, too!

(He does so. Music fades out.)

(John feels faint and sits down suddenly. He rubs his head.)

JOHN
Whoops. Feelin' a bit of a sinkin' spell, I believe.

CATHERINE
John, what is it?

JESSE
You under the weather, Host? I didn't wanna say anything but you do look a little peaked.

(The three children notice that John has suddenly taken to the chase. They stop what they're doing and go to him in concern.)

CATHERINE
He did have an upset stomach this mornin'.

MARGUERITE
What's the matter with Da?

JESSE
Let's get him some water.

(Someone does.)

CATHERINE
Elevate his feet. Your Da's ok. Just over-heated a bit. Alright now, you three off to your bedrooms ta spruce 'em up. Go on, now. He'll be fine. Go on now!

(The three go into their requisite doorways to the bedrooms. Music slowly fades out.)

JESSE
Host, there's just a little something I thought I should mention to you and Catherine.

JOHN
Any problem?

JESSE
No,... I mean, I'm not real sure,...yet.

CATHERINE
What is it, Jesse?

JESSE
I'm sure it's nothing.

JOHN
Don't tell me its termites already.

JESSE
No, no. Nothing like that. The structure is sound, she's built like an ox. I saw to that myself.

CATHERINE
Well, tell us.

JESSE
Some sounds.

JOHN
Sounds?

JESSE
Maybe just a slight plumbing issue. Could even be a racoon running loose.

CATHERINE
Where is it, Jesse?

JESSE
Beneath your floorboard. Right over about here. A few times,… When giving it all a once over,… I started hearing something like it was coming from the foundation.

JOHN
The house is settling, maybe?

JESSE
No, first it's like uh, … a beating sort of, like maybe air in the pipes, or could be valves.

CATHERINE
You don't suppose a poor squirrel got caught between the boards.

JESSE
I don't know. Could be. It's localized. I don't hear it come from any other part of the house. Just this area here. Right after the bumping noise, it's a strange sound like a heavy branch being slowly broken in half. You know like wood being split or…. I don't know. Tell you what, tomorrow morning, I'll go under and see what's what. I'll clear it all up tomorrow.

JOHN
I'm sure you will.

JESSE
Thank you, my Host.

CATHERINE
No, Jesse, thank you.

JESSE
Well, listen. I'll just grab my tools and go. I'll leave you to your new home. I know you'll be happy here. Welcome to the neighborhood.

JOHN
Thanks, Jesse.

(Jesse exits by the front door.)

JOHN
Huh. Squirrels and racoons. Maybe I've caught
a mild case of the rabies from them.

CATHERINE
Oh stop.

JOHN
The requisite groans of a new home.

CATHERINE
Yes, there are worse problems we could have. Tea time?

JOHN
Tea time.

(Music in. They exit into the kitchen.)

[End of Scene]

Scene 2

"Benediction"

(Music from the previous scene plays through to the next. Light outside the quarter moon windows upstairs gradually rises to indicate morning. Thomas enters and addresses the audience.)

THOMAS

The next day, it came time to have the house blessed. Ma had sent a letter to the local diocese months previous. They'd sent a Father Garrett Fitzgerald. I had just gotten a brand new camera. I had a school project and hoped that the good Father would allow me to photograph the ceremony.

(Thomas exits. A doorbell is heard. The chimes at the end of the song can very well work for this sound effect. John and Catherine enter and go to the front door to answer. Music fades out. They open the door. Father Garret Fitzgerald, in full priestly garb, is revealed at the door.)

FATHER FITZGERALD
Mr. and Mrs. Moynahan?

JOHN
Yes, that's us all right.

CATHERINE
You must be our priest? Father Fitzgerald?

FATHER FITZGERALD
Guilty on both counts.

(All laugh)

CATHERINE
Come in, come in!

JOHN
I'm John and this is Catherine.

FATHER FITZGERALD
A pleasure to make your acquaintance, finally.

(He shakes hands with John while Catherine goes toward the hallway door.)

CATHERINE
Eileen! Thomas!

JOHN
We appreciate your comin' out on such short notice.

FATHER FITZGERALD
Not a problem at all. It comes with the proverbial territory.

CATHERINE
Occupational hazard, ya might say?

FATHER FITZGERALD
Aye, yes, indeed.

CATHERINE
May I take your hat and coat?

FATHER FITZGERALD
Why, thank you.

(Catherine helps Father Fitzgerald off with his things. She hangs up the priest's coat and hat on a coat rack in a corner near the front door while John chats Garret up.)

JOHN
So, you're from the Sacred Heart Parochial House.

FATHER FITZGERALD
Suffolk County Sacred Heart, yes. But, as opposed to "Parochial House" back home, here in the states we just call it a rectory. Been there for a few years now.

CATHERINE
It's a beautiful place, nonetheless.

FATHER FITZGERALD
That it is.

JOHN
Then you would know Father Giovanni.

FATHER FITZGERALD
I certainly do!

CATHERINE
How is he fairin'?

FATHER FITZGERALD
Oh, fine. Fine.

JOHN
And his lumbago?

FATHER FITZGERALD
Well, not as much pain as before. It comes and goes, as ya know. But he's in good spirits, in good hands.

CATHERINE
I love your accent. Unusual. What part of Ireland are ya from?

JOHN
It's certainly not Dublin.

(They laugh)

FATHER FITZGERALD
No, no. Not Dublin. *(He laughs)* Lisburn, County Down. In the northern part of the country, as ya know.

CATHERINE
Well, that would explain it.

(Garret begins opening his attache case and pulls out the necessary implements for the blessing of the house.)

FATHER FITZGERALD
In sooth, my family's lived all over, which makes our dialect somewhat of a mixed stock in the great pot of stew.

JOHN
Well put, well put…

(Eileen and Thomas enter. Eileen has done up her hair and freshened her make-up. Thomas is carrying in his camera equipment.)

JOHN
And there they are!

FATHER FITZGERALD
Ahh, who've we here?

CATHERINE
Two of our children. Eileen and Thomas.

(Thomas shakes hands with Garret.)

THOMAS
I'm Thomas.

FATHER FITZGERALD
Yes, I put two and two together. I didn't think you were Eileen.

(Eileen steps forward and takes Garret by the hand. It is clear that she is taken by Garret's handsome looks.)

EILEEN
And I'm Eileen.

FATHER FITZGERALD
A pleasure to meet you, Eileen.

~ AMITYVILLE 1925 ~

EILEEN
Eileen Moynahan.

FATHER FITZGERALD
Yes. I gathered you were a Moynahan.

(She continues holding on to Garret's hand with a fixed smile as she locks eyes with him. She never looks away from his face. She is transfixed. The moment becomes awkward as it appears she won't let go of his hand.)

JOHN
Eileen, Dear. You can let go now.

(John helps to separate their hands.)

Father Fitzgerald needs his hand to toss the holy water, Dear.

(Embarrassed, Eileen's spell is broken and she finally lets go.)

EILEEN
Oh, dear, yes, yes, of course. Terribly sorry. I do that all the time when I meet someone so,... That is,... so,...

THOMAS
Priestly?

EILEEN
I do that all the time. I have,... a tendancy... ta extend handshakes a bit longer than,... necessary.

THOMAS
(With obvious sarcasm)

Oh, yes, all the time. Big problem with this one, it is. Listen, Father, I have a school project on photography. Would ya mind terribly if I documented the blessing with pictures?

FATHER FITZGERALD
Oh, that'd be fine. Take as many as ya like.

CATHERINE
Thank ya, Father. Very kind of ya.

FATHER FITZGERALD
Is this the whole family?

JOHN
No, we've got a middle child. Marguerite. But she's not feelin' quite herself today so, we're lettin' her stay in bed till she feels less peak-ed.

FATHER FITZGERALD
Sorry ta hear that. Give her my best. Now, we can stand in a circle, if ya like.

(Gentle piano eases in as Eileen breaks away from the group momentarily and crosses downstage to share with the audience. During her monologue, Garret goes through the silent motions of reading from his book and officiating the blessing ceremony.)

EILEEN
So, Father Garret Fitzgerald began. In Irish Catholic tradition, it is customary for the entire family to be present. But as Marguerite apparently had a difficult night, she slept in and we said a family prayer over her. As the Father's ceremony was drawin' to a close, I couldn't help but notice how lovely he looked in his frocked collar. By the way,

it didn't hurt that he was a handsome young man... Quite handsome, indeed!

(She gives a cheeky smile as she turns and goes back to join the ceremony. All this time, Thomas has been snapping photographs of Father Fitzgerald.)

FATHER FITZGERALD
(As he sprinkles those present, and the home with holy water)

Let this water call ta mind
Our baptism into Christ
Who has redeemed us by
His death and resurrection.

ALL
Amen.

FATHER FITZGERALD
May the peace of Christ rule in our hearts,
And may the word of Christ in all its richness
Dwell in us. So that whatever we do in
Word and in work, we will do in the name
Of the Lord.

ALL
Amen.

(Garret sings the following Latin verse)

FATHER FITZGERALD
"Iam ut totam convertere diaboli
Ceremonia est a falsum actio
Itaque ut domum beati non est a Christo

Sed a principe tenebrarum
In aeternum in maledictione
Reputabitur. Sic fiat semper.
Amen."

ALL
Amen.

JOHN
It's a shame Marguerite couldn't be here ta listen to the Latin. She studies it, understands it, and loves it so.

CATHERINE
I just love to hear the name of Jesus in Latin. 'Christo'. It's beautiful, isn't it, Father?

FATHER FITZGERALD
Yes, it is, Mrs. Moynahan. To speak the lord's name in any language is a blessin' to the priest.

(A gentle piano eases in as John crosses downstage to address the audience. He starts speaking immediately and the following activity is done in silence upstage of him; Garret packs up his kit and there is a pantomime of Eileen offering a cup of tea to the priest. He is seen turning it down. Thomas takes his time packing up his photography gear. Catherine goes to the coat rack to retrieve Garret's coat. Eileen takes it and helps Garret into the sleeves.

JOHN
The blessing given and niceties exchanged, Eileen offered a cup o' tea to Father Fitzgerald. He refused, as he had a funeral to officiate within the hour and had to be on his way. Thomas had taken plenty of photographs for his school project and carefully put everything away. We felt a collective

sigh of peace and relief. The blessing, we believed, would make our house, a holy home.

(Music fades out as John turns his attention back to Garret)

Sorry ya can't stay for tea, Father.

FATHER FITZGERALD
I'll take a rain check, for certain. But thank you all. Oh, and here's the number where I can be reached. *(He takes out a small piece of paper and hands it to Catherine.)*

CATHERINE
Oh, thank you, father. You're welcome here, any time.

EILEEN
You can say that again.

FATHER FITZGERALD
I beg your pardon?

EILEEN
Oh, I said, please come back and visit when ya can.

(John opens the door for Garret. He shakes his hand.)

JOHN
Thanks again and give my best to Father Giovanni.

FATHER FITZGERALD
I'll do so. And I'll say a little prayer for Marguerite. Hope she's on the mend, soon. Peace be with ye all.

ALL
And also with you.

(Father Fitzgerald exits, leaving behind his hat. Eileen notices, grabs it from the coat rack and goes to the threshold.)

EILEEN
Father Fitzgerald! Wait! Your hat!

(Eileen exits after him. John closes the front door and laughs. Catherine notices a small pile of Thomas' odds and ends on a nearby table. This includes a loose deck of cards, his hat, and camera equipment.)

CATHERINE
Well, would ya just look at all this? Thomas, please pick up your things. And John you'd better go have a lie-down. *(She feels his forehead.)* Appears ya have another spell comin' on. Go on.

JOHN
Yes, Florence Nightingale.

(He exits up the stairs. Catherine and Thomas are straightening the living room. Suddenly a blast of frightening music, wall sconces begin flickering, a chair slides and slams into a wall, a picture slides from side to side on a wall, and the deck of cards begins fountaining upward. Upstairs, John is oblivious to the paranormal activity. Catherine and Thomas are shocked, scream, and physically jolted backward. Suddenly, the chaos and music stops. There is a pause while Catherine and Thomas attempt to process what they've just experienced.)

THOMAS
Ma,... did ya see that?

CATHERINE
I saw it, Thomas.

THOMAS
It scared me half-blind.

CATHERINE
Me too.

THOMAS
I think a glass shattered. Nearly cut my leg, but didn't.

CATHERINE
Did ya tear your pants?

THOMAS
That's not all I did in my pants.

CATHERINE
There's a perfectly reasonable explanation for this.

THOMAS
Like what, Ma?

CATHERINE
A draft in the house?

THOMAS
(Unconvinced)
Ok.

CATHERINE
Now, let's gather these things together and put them away.

THOMAS
You first.

(Catherine helps to pick up a tea cup and saucer and heads to the kitchen. Thomas picks up the cards, puts them in his hat, grabs his camera and heads to his room. Music continues to play, bridging into the next scene.)

[End of Scene]

Scene 3

"Darkness Manifest"

(Music fades from the previous scene to ease the transition. John, Catherine, and Thomas exit. Marguerite enters to a period popular song on the turntable. She carries a tray with a large silver spoon, fork and large butcher knife. She begins cleaning each one with a fluid and cloth. When she gets to the butcher knife she pays particular and odd attention to the sharp point. She gazes at her reflection in the blade. The doorbell rings. She keeps the knife in her hand. She goes to the front door. It is Jesse Purdy.)

MARGUERITE
Oh Mr. Purdy, won't you come in?

JESSE
How are you feeling, Marguerite?

MARGUERITE
Not quite myself yet, but better, I suppose.

JESSE
I just came by to check out the foundation. I need to have a look at the floorboards in your living room.

MARGUERITE
Of course, Mr. Purdy. Help yourself.

JESSE
Thank you.

(Jesse goes over to the living room center, peels back the rug and runs his hands over the floor to see if there has been any residual buckling from moisture. He puts on his glasses and takes a closer look at the boards. He takes a mason jar out of his tool box. The jar has a horizontal distinct line painted across it's center. He uses this as a level. He places it at different points on the floor boards.)

MARGURERITE
Need any help?

JESSE
No, dear, thank you. I'm just going to check for buckling or moisture. Make sure everything's still level here. (A beat.) You have a beautiful family. And your father, "the Host" is a great man.

MARGUERITE
We think so, too.

JESSE
I admire him a lot. So, Marguerite,...

MARGUERITE
Yes, Mr. Purdy?

JESSE
You like what I've done with the house?

MARGUERITE
Why do ya ask that?

JESSE
Well, you're the only one I haven't heard from yet about your new home.

MARGUERITE
You've done a great job, Mr. Purdy. It's a fine house. And I'm sorry if I hadn't expressed that ta ya till now.

JESSE
No, it's ok. I guess I'm just fishing for compliments, haha.

MARGUERITE
Mr. Purdy, may I be perfectly honest with ya? No blarney. Just the God's honest truth.

JESSE
Well, of course. What is it, Marguerite?

MARGUERITE
It's nothin' ta do with you. I'm not placin' blame.

JESSE
Tell me.

MARGUERITE
Somethin's not right here. From the moment I stepped over the threshold, I felt, I don't exactly how ta describe it. 'Threatened', I suppose. Yes, that's it. Like the house or somethin' within its walls doesn't want us here. I know it sounds crazy. You must think me mad. But, today,...

JESSE
Yes?

(Music of mysterious nature eases in gradually, almost imperceptibly and builds in intensity throughout the rest of the scene.)

MARGUERITE
I felt the spirit of somethin' very old was tryin' to reach me. Ta tell me somethin'. Somethin,... evil. And the moment I felt this churnin' in my soul, I could swear I heard a voice whisperin' ta me... in French. It said,...

(Marguarite's personality seems to morph into something unGodly.)

MARGUERITE
"Vous et votre famille etes des passeurs, dans la maison du diable. Quitter ou brule en enfer pour toujours."

JESSE
What does that mean?

MARGUERITE
You and your family are trespassers in the house of the devil. Leave or burn in Hell forever.

JESSE
Maybe,... Maybe you've not been feeling well? Or sometimes, the wind off the creek can make sounds, like whispering voices. I've had that experience myself. You just need rest. It's been a long day for you. It's hard adjusting to a new home.

MARGUERITE
What the fuck do you know about it?

JESSE
What? Marguerite?

MARGUERITE
She's not here at present.

JESSE
What are you talking about?

MARGUERITE
Marguerite is not home. She's visitin' dear friends. *(She uses the knife to punctuate).* They live there. Under the house. In the floorboards.

JESSE
Well, I've got a lot to do. I think it's time for me to head home.

MARGUERITE
Don't go Jesse Purdy. We've so much to say to you. And to show you.

JESSE
I'll just gather my tools.

(At this moment, lights in the house flicker. One by one, pictures on the wall begin to move about. They slide against the wall, to and fro. A pounding from the floorboards begins softly then increases in volume. A dining chair slides across the floor and slams into a wall. Marguerite spreads her arms wide as though causing the chaos about her. Jesse is stunned, he goes over to the center of the living room where the pounding is heard under the floorboards. He stares at it in disbelief for a moment. All of a sudden, Marguerite lowers her arms. Music and everything supernatural stops. Marguerite has returned to her normal self. She goes back to cleaning up. A pause.)

MARGUARITE
Leaving now, Mr. Purdy?

JESSE
Yes. I'll come back in the morning and check the crawlspace. Sounds like you've got something in the pipes. That's all. That's all it is. I'll fix it tomorrow.

MARGUERITE

You know what's down there. *(She points the knife threateningly at Purdy.)* Don't ya, Mr. Purdy?

JESSE

Like I said, it's late. I should go.

MARGUARITE

Goodnight, Mr. Purdy.

JESSE

Goodnight, Marguerite. I'll just show myself out. Get some,... rest.

(Jesse exits. Strange and demonic whispering can be heard from the center of the floor. Marguerite gazes at the area as though receiving information and commands from some unseen entity. Marguerite, as if in a trance, glides slowly to the tray, places the knife upon it and exits back through the door of the kitchenl. Exits. Music continues as lights fade a bit. A sudden flash of lighting and crash of thunder.)

[End of Scene]

Scene 4

"The Inconvenience of Chastity"

(Night. It has begun to rain outside. Lightning and thunder. Music from the previous scene bridges into the opening of the front door. Enter Eileen and Father Fitzgerald. They rush in, crossing the threshold to avoid getting dowsed by the coming deluge. Father Fitzgerald folds up his umbrella. They both shake off a little water from their hair. They brush off droplets from their shoulders. As they close the door, there is a single flash of lightning followed by a distant roll of thunder.)

EILEEN
Whew! It's on its way!

FATHER FITZGERALD
It *is* that! Where shall I stow this?

(He refers to his umbrella.)

EILEEN
Here in the corner.

(She refers to an antique milk can.)

We use it as an umbrella stand. Reminds us of the old country.
(Garret places the dripping umbrella in its place to dry. Music gradually fades out.)

FATHER FITZGERALD
Does me as well. Well, Eileen, that was a most eventful trip to the library, don't ya agree?

EILEEN
(Laughs)

That it was. That it was. I don't think I've ever been 'shushed' by such an intimidating battalion of librarians in all my life.

FATHER FITZGERALD
My word! Weren't they the most frightenin' brigade of ninety-year old matrons?

EILEEN
Oh, I think we could've taken 'em. It's all in the element of surprise, ya know.

FATHER FITZGERALD
Don't let librarians fool ya, Eileen. They're all loaded for bear. Those grandmas have a mean left hook. They'll give Jack Dempsey a run for his money!

EILEEN
(Laughs)

And they've got weapons. If you're not careful ya can get pummeled by an errant card catalogue!

FATHER FITZGERALD
Good one!
(They laugh.)

EILEEN
Father Fitz, may I offer ya a cup o' tea?

FATHER FITZGERALD
Thanks much. But I really should be goin'. It's gettin' late and I don't want ta disturb your folks.

EILEEN
They're all up ta kip by now. Fast asleep, they are… Deep sleepers. *(Awkward pause)* What say ya stay just long enough for your umbrella ta dry out? And maybe by then the storm'll pass over.

FATHER FITZGERALD
Well,… all right then. One cup o' tea and I'm off.

EILEEN
Agreed.
(Eileen goes to the kitchen to prepare a cup of tea.)

What'll ya have? We've got Lyon's, Barrys, Bewleys?

FATHER FITZGERALD
Barrys is fine, thank ya.

EILEEN
Most popular tea in Ireland, it is.

FATHER FITZGERALD
Indeed. How'd ya find it here?

EILEEN
We brought some over.

FATHER FITZGERALD
Good job, that.

(Eileen goes to the kitchen. She speaks to Father Fitzgerald as she gathers the tea. Father Fitzgerald sits on the wingback chair.)

EILEEN
Ya mentioned Jack Dempsey. Do ya follow the rows?

FATHER FITZGERALD
Oh, yes. Gene Tunney's in Philly. Dempsey's everywhere. Pretty soon promoters will bring those two together again, just mark my words.

(Eileen brings a cup with saucer and tea bag to Garret.)

EILEEN
Water was hot already.

FATHER FITZGERALD
Thanks much.

EILEEN
Hope it's all right.

(He sips.)

FATHER FITZGERALD
Well it's just perfect, is what it is. Thank ya, Dear.

EILEEN
You're always welcome, Father.

(Eileen crosses to the Victrola.)

FATHER FITZGERALD
Nice talking machine.

EILEEN
Thanks. It's a Gramophone. Want ta hear somethin' new?

FATHER FITZGERALD
Sure!

EILEEN
It's already on the turn-table. Been playin' it
over and over down to the grooves.

FATHER FITZGERALD
Must be good, all right.

(She winds up the machine, then sets the needle on the vinyl. The song begins. It is 1925's "Nights When I Am Lonely" by the Boswell Sisters. Eileen gets into the music. Her body moves to the song. Father Fitzgerald enjoys it as well.)

EILEEN
They're called 'The Boswell Sisters'. This one is "Nights When I am Lonely". It just makes me want ta move. How they can swing.

FATHER FITZGERALD
Yes, they can swing all right.

EILEEN
They rest of it just gets a bit silly.

(She turns the volume down a bit.)

You *do* like music?

FATHER FITZGERALD
Love it.

EILEEN
Don't ya just love Irving Berlin?

FATHER FITZGERALD
Berlin's good. Tell ya the truth, I prefer Gershwin.

EILEEN
Oh, a Gershwin man! I love his work too!

FATHER FITZGERALD
What is it about Gershwin, I wonder?

EILEEN
Well,... I think that,... His is the sound of the American dream, ya know. The heartbeat of industry. The power of engines, sweat of a man's brow. Molten steel quickened, then riveted into scaffolding. And girders swaying in a Manhattan skyline… Forgive me. I'm just a foolish, sentimental sot. I don't have a clue what I'm talkin' about.

FATHER FITZGERALD
That's not true, Eileen. You know precisely what you're talkin' about. That's why I enjoy your company.

EILEEN
May I ask you a question?

FATHER FITZGERALD
I believe ya just did.

EILEEN
No, I mean a real question.

FATHER FITZGERALD
Of course.

EILEEN
Have ya never kissed a girl?

FATHER FITZGERALD
Does my mother count?

EILEEN
No. I mean a *real* girl.

FATHER FITZGERALD
Oh, a *real* girl. No. Not much experience with kissin'. When I entered the priesthood, Bishop O'Malley held a large crucifix in front of me. I knelt down and was instructed to kiss the wooden feet of Christ. Before that, I'd not kissed an inanimate object since my family's visit to the blarney stone.

EILEEN
Well, kissin' the blarney stone is not exactly where I was goin' with this.

(A flash of lightning followed by a sudden loud crash of thunder. They both dart towards the windows to look outside.)

It's a deluge. It's pouring.

(Father Fitz looks out another window.)

FATHER FITZGERALD
Oh my. I'll get swept away in the flood for certain.

EILEEN
Ya can't go out there tonight.

FATHER FITZGERALD
I guess not.

EILEEN
So,… spend the night on the chaise.

(Eileen goes to a cabinet to fetch a pillow and blanket.)

FATHER FITZGERALD
Oh no, I couldn't do that.

EILEEN
Why not?

FATHER FITZGERALD
Honestly, I don't want to impose.

EILEEN
You'll not be imposin'. We're happy to have ya.

FATHER FITZGERALD
You're certain it's all right.

EILEEN
It's perfectly fine. I won't take 'no' for an answer.

FATHER FITZGERALD
Well,… maybe just a few hours. But then as soon as the storm passes, I must be on my way.

EILEEN
Fine.

(As Eileen arranges his makeshift bed, Father Fitzgerald addresses the audience.)

FATHER FITZGERALD
It was clear that if I ventured out into a night like this, I'd never make it to the rectory in one piece. After a bit of back and forth, Eileen convinced me to sleep on the chaise lounge. At least until the storm let up.

EILEEN
The pillow is soft, the blanket warm, and if ya need anything, just make yourself ta home.

FATHER FITZGERALD
Please don't make a fuss.

(Eileen places his tea cup and books on a small table near the chaise.)

EILEEN
You'll have your tea right here. Your books, if you'd like to read by candlelight. I'll hang up your jacket.

(Eileen hangs up his jacket.)

FATHER FITZGERALD
Thank you, Eileen. God bless.

EILEEN
Amen… Father, ya know my favorite verse from the Boswell Sisters?

FATHER FITZGERALD
What's that?

EILEEN
"Nights when I feel lonely, nights when I feel blue, I think of you only, for no one else will do"… *(Loud thunderclap.)* Goodnight, Father.

FATHER FITZGERALD
Goodnight, Eileen.

(Father Fitz lays his head upon the pillow and closes his eyes as Eileen turns down the intensity of a nearby lamp and the lights fade to a lower level. Lightning flashes through windows, casting ominous and anthropomorphic shadows. Eileen exits.)

[End of Scene]

Scene 5

"Naked Fear"

(Music carries over from previous scene and plays through to the end. Living room is darkened. Father Fitzgerald is asleep. Ominous frightening music eases in. The door to Marguerite's bedroom hallway slowly opens and a paranormal light rises from the portal. A hand sticks out holding a fully-lit gothic candelabra. Marguerite, wearing nightgown and bathrobe enters from that light in a trance. She strolls about the room, crawls over the settee, then crawls around to the backside of the chaise. She hides. She slowly pulls his blanket off of him as though it is being removed by invisible hands. Marguerite then reaches her hands, claw-like, above the back of the chaise like a scene from "Nosferatu". She then raises her face from the back and gazes at the Father asleep on the chaise. She crawls on top it to straddle him. All the while, Marguerite's movement is underscored and punctuated by a spectacular show of lightning flashes and deafening thunderclaps. Father Fitz awakens to see Marguerite staring at his only inches away from his face. He is shocked.)

MARGUERITE
Wakey Wakey!

(He throws her off of him.)

FATHER FITZGERALD
Who are ya!?

MARGUERITE
Ya know full well who I am.

FATHER FITZGERALD
Well, ya must be… Marguerite?

MARGUERITE
Marguerite isn't here at present.

FATHER FITZGERALD
You're sleep-walkin', lass. Go back to bed.

MARGUERITE
I'd rather curl up here on the sofa with you.

FATHER FITZGERALD
No! Now, you turn around this instant and leave me alone!

MARGUERITE
But I've just arrived. Don't you want to see what I've brought you?

(Marguerite drops her robe to the floor revealing her nightgown.)

MARGUERITE
Behold, the body and blood of Christ.

FATHER FITZGERALD
Put on that robe, blasphemer!

MARGUERITE
I've been awful naughty, Priest. And I need to be spanked. Would you like ta spank my bare bottom?

FATHER FITZGERALD
I'll not be given to pleasures of the flesh.

(Suddenly, the sound of thunder fades, lightning continues to flash and the strange sounds of creaking come from the center of the floor and grab Marguerite's attention.)

MARGUERITE
There's something alive under this house.

FATHER FITZGERALD
Get dressed! Go away!

MARGUERITE
The corpse of little Agatha has been moving, clawing, writhing about. She's been trying to break through the floor, but she's young and frail. And she needs help. Agatha has a warning for our family.

FATHER FITZGERALD
You're a foul denizen of Hell.

MARGUERITE
Her coffin is so small, and cold. She can hardly breathe in there. She needs you ta help her out of it.

MARGUERITE
Have ya never embraced the reeking corpse of a dead child? Felt her cold, stiffened bones brown from rot? Have ya never gazed into her milky-white eyes? A droplet of blood running from her dry, blue lips? Felt her awaken until she smiled and began to giggle softly? Until the giggle turned into a laugh, and the laugh became the sound of a million persecuted souls burning in Hell?

(Father Fitzgerald goes to his jacket and puts it on.)

FATHER FITZGERALD
You're asleep I tell ya. Dreamin'. Go back ta bed!

(He grabs his cloak and hat.)

MARGUERITE
Agatha's waitin' for ya.

FATHER FITZGERALD
LIES!

MARGUERITE
Cradle her.

(Father Fitzgerald goes to the front door.)

FATHER FITZGERALD
God's mercy and power reign o'er your soul!

MARGUERITE
Go to her, Priest. Let little Agatha out of her coffin.

(Father Fitzgerald swings open the front door then bolts out into the damp night. Marguerite puts on her robe, looks back down at the floorboards and exits into her hallway. Music becomes evil.)

[End of Scene]

Scene 6

"This House Doesn't Want Us"

(Music from previous scene leads into this. Thomas enters the kitchen from the bedrooms-hallway door. Catherine awakes as she has heard Thomas. She notices John is not in bed. She finds a note left on John's pillow. She reads it. She quickly dresses and goes downstairs to encounter Thomas in the kitchen. He has a book in his hands. He sets it on the table, slices a piece of soda bread, sits down, and while eating opens the book to read silently. Catherine enters kitchen. Music fades out as soon as Catherine speaks.)

CATHERINE
Ahhh, soda bread. Well, isn't that the breakfast of champions.

THOMAS
(Unenthusiastically)
Top 'o the mornin', Ma.

CATHERINE
So, how'd ya sleep?

THOMAS
Not at all.

CATHERINE
Neither did your Da.

THOMAS
I heard him tossin' up his guts.

| 45

CATHERINE
Don't be crude.

THOMAS
Middle 'o the night, I heard him.

CATHERINE
He didn't sleep at all. And yet he's out at the crack 'o dawn this mornin' doin' God only knows. Left this note sayin' he left with Mr. Purdy ta pick up pesticide for the hedges. But somethin's not right.

THOMAS
Da's gettin' worse, isn't he?

CATHERINE
We all are. It's this house. The house doesn't want us here.

THOMAS
I think I know what's happenin' with this place.

CATHERINE
What is it?

THOMAS
There's a reason I was up all night.

CATHERINE
What do ya mean, Thomas?

THOMAS
I was readin' this, cover ta cover. Couldn't put it down. I studied it.

CATHERINE
What is it, exactly?

THOMAS
Here, read the title.

CATHERINE
"The Dark Art Of Cursing A Home In The Name Of And With The Powers Wielded By Lucifer Himself"... What is this?

THOMAS
Well, don't ya see, Ma? That's what's goin' on.

CATHERINE
What is?

THOMAS
This would explain the strange occurrences. The deck of cards flyin' about, the sounds from the floor, chairs and tables movin' of their own accord, candles floatin' in the middle of the night...

CATHERINE
Your Da gettin' so sick...

THOMAS
The Victorola playin' by itself.

CATHERINE
And all after the house had been properly blessed.
Under the good Lord's protection.

THOMAS

Ma, blessin's by priests have been known ta be invalidated through demonic means. All it takes is a concerted effort by those who intend ta curse or unknowingly open a portal.

CATHERINE

And how is it you know so much about such things?

THOMAS

I told ya'. I've been makin' a study. I stayed up
till the crow 'o the cock devourin' this.

CATHERINE

Maybe ya need not look at such things.

THOMAS

Maybe ya need ta ask Eileen why she had this
God-forsaken thing in the first place.

CATHERINE

Eileen? What was she doin' with such a book?

THOMAS

I don't know. But I found it in the loo just after she'd finished in there. And I know it wasn't there before because I'd just brushed my teeth prior ta her goin' in. I didn't see it then. It's Eileen's all right. She's up ta somethin', Ma.

CATHERINE

I just don't believe it. It doesn't make sense. Eileen would never involve herself in such hocus-pocus.

THOMAS
I'm not suggestin' she's doin' anythin' on purpose. I'm sayin' books like this, especially by that Mr. Crowley, are dangerous.

CATHERINE
What's in it? What does it say?

THOMAS
Just listen ta this… *(He turns to a specific passage and reads aloud.)* "Beware of those followers of Christ who may attempt to thwart your intent to curse the home. For they are adversaries of our great and powerful prince of darkness. They shall use the holy word of their God to extinguish the fires of Hell on Earth that you yourself summon. Use caution and beware.

The most opportune time to break your curse or exorcise demonic possession on a home is sooner than later. Within the first two days of residence is ideal. This is due to the nature of our evil having to quicken over forty-eight hours, not unlike a plaster of paris cast on a fractured arm…"

CATHERINE
Let me see that. (Thomas hands the book to Catherine. She reads aloud.) "The third day, however, of any household possession by evil spirits is significant as it is an established tradition by the devil and his denizens to mock the three-fold dynamic symbolized by the holy trinity; the Father, the Son, and the Holy Ghost."

(The lights in the wall sconces begin to go off, then back on again. A wooden kitchen chair suddenly slides across the floor, slams into a wall, and shatters into pieces and splinters. A loud and horrible sound like metal ripping through metal peels out in an ear-spitting volume. The two quarter moon windows upstairs suddenly open. Sconce lights flash again and the cabinet doors in the kitchen fly open.)

CATHERINE
Let's go, Thomas!

THOMAS
Where?

CATHERINE
We're going for a little ride.

(She quickly grabs her coat and car keys)

THOMAS
Where to?

CATHERINE
The Amityville Historical Society. It won't hurt ta do a little diggin'.

THOMAS
Now you're talkin'.

CATHERINE
I want ta find out more about who lived in the Ireland's house on this property before this one was built. Your Da probably took the Chrysler. We'll take the Model A.

(She checks to make sure she has the right keys then heads swiftly to the door.)

THOMAS
Well, don't leave without me.

CATHERINE
Come, Thomas, we need ta go now!

THOMAS
But I've not finished my soda bread.

CATHERINE
You'll finish it along the way. The faster we take action, the quicker we can save our family.

THOMAS
According to the book, we're nearly out of time.

CATHERINE
Leave that thing alone. And not a word of this to your father. We don't want anythin' to upset him further.

THOMAS
Got it.

CATHERINE
Good boy. Now close the door behind ya.

THOMAS
Yes, Ma.

CATHERINE
They're not going ta take away my husband. They're not going ta take away my home.

(She exits. Thomas goes back to the table to retrieve what's left of his slice of soda bread.)

THOMAS

They're not goin' ta take away my soda bread, I can promise ya that!

(Music in, as Thomas exits after Catherine. Marguerite enters and addresses the audience.)

MARGUERITE

In the house at 112 Ocean Avenue, time began to lose all meanin'. It was as if the grandfather's clock jumped us all from hour to hour. Nine o'clock in the mornin' inexplicably lapsed into three am. Ma heard the sound of a crying child emanating from the kitchen. She went to investigate while Da had night terrors. *(Exit)*

[End of Scene]

Scene 7

"The Noose Tightens"

(Music leads in from previous scene. Night time lighting. "It's Three O' Clock in the Morning" cranks up again to signal three am. This wakes John up. As if in a trance, he puts on his robe and slowly descends the stairs. He goes to the Victrola to turn off the song. Immediately, we hear the loud sound of rope being pulled by weight. It is the sound of a hangman's line suddenly being drawn taught. Ambient, foreboding music eases in to underscore the entire scene following. Catherine stirs, puts her robe on, quickly goes to the top of the stairs. The moment she sees John, she senses something is urgently wrong. She picks up the telephone on a small table. She dials a number. We see her wait a moment. She is then seen speaking into the receiver, but she cannot be heard. She has called Father Fitzgerald to urge him to come to the house. John goes to the tool wall and takes the scythe. He crosses to center stage and gazes up with absolute terror at the upper rafters of the house. His gaze is fixed, his body becomes still as a stone statue. By this point, Catherine has already descended the stairs, and into the living room to meet John who is standing strangely. He is clearly transfixed by something no one else can see.)

CATHERINE
John? Darlin'? What's the matter?

(No answer.)

John, love, what are ya doin' with the scythe?
Answer me, John. What's happenin'?

JOHN
(Still staring at the ceiling)
Do ya remember last year in Fedamore, County Limerick? That widow they found guilty of murder?

CATHERINE
Yes. Annie Walsh.

JOHN
She slaughtered her husband Ned in their own home with a hatchet. During Sowein. I think she's in this house.

CATHERINE
John, you're having a night terror. Let me warm up a nice glass of milk for ya. And then ya come back ta bed.

(John breaks his gaze from the ceiling to look at Catherine. He appears to see right through her.)

JOHN
No, Catherine. I don't want warm milk. This house is tainted. It's spoiled. Gone off. This place is tryin' ta send us a message.

CATHERINE
I know. We're goin' to cleanse it, John. Together. I promise. Eileen checked out a book from the library. All about the cursing of houses. Look at what Thomas and I found at the historical society this afternoon. *(She goes to a drawer to retrieve a small stack of papers.)* This property was once owned by a man named John Ketcham. Here's the proof, right here in these papers. Thomas and I then went to the library. Look at this document. Ketcham was a witch who'd tortured Indians and vowed that this land would be cursed forever.

He was an evil man, John. This says here that he murdered his own daughter, Agatha Ketcham. I think its her spirit dwells on this property. She's angry we're here. She can't rest. But love, don't worry. We'll not let this thing defeat us.

JOHN

Agatha Ketcham. Yes, she's here too. We ran into each other earlier today. She came in, uninvited, ya might say.

CATHERINE

What are ya talkin' about?

JOHN

Nevermind. It's too late. Just like it was too late for Ned Walsh, Annie's dead husband. She was having an affair with Ned's nephew, Michael Talbot. Remember? They were fucking one another.

CATHERINE

John, I don't understand what this has ta do with anythin'. Just put that thing down and…

JOHN

So then the lovers decided that Ned Walsh was standin' in the way of their happiness. In the way of their repugnant, putrid and fetid trysts of ungodly fornication and sodomy.

CATHERINE

John, I want ya ta stop this now. Put down the scythe and let's go to the kitchen for a nice cup o' tea. It will help ya ta sleep.

JOHN

Oh, I'll not sleep. It's not… *safe* ta sleep in this place.

CATHERINE

Darlin',…

JOHN

So they went out to the tool shed and Michael found a rusted old hatchet, splintery wooden handle, blade still sharp as a razor… And I'll bet ya remember what happened next.

CATHERINE

Let's not talk about this now. You're in no condition.

JOHN

Annie crept up to her sleeping husband. She wrenched that hatchet right out of Michael's hand and she hacked and hacked and hacked away at Ned's neck until his throat opened like a zipper.

CATHERINE

Ya really need to stop this.

JOHN

At her sentencing, the barrister argued. "She's a lady. So, go light on her." Ya remember what happened. Yes?

CATHERINE

Yes, they executed her, anyways.

JOHN

That they did. They led her out to the town square. On the early morn of October 31st, 1924, they hung her like a slaughtered pig.

CATHERINE

Give me the scythe, John. You're dreamin'.

JOHN
No. Annie Walsh really *is* in this house.

CATHERINE
If she's here, where is she? Point to her, John. Show me.

JOHN
There she is. Up there. Swingin' from the rafters. You see her, don't you? Right above us.

CATHERINE
There's no one there, John. Listen to me. We've got ta get help.

JOHN
Help, yes, help. The hangin' nearly popped her head clear off. Ya can see where the rope is so tight about her neck, it cut its way in, and got a strangle-hold around her windpipe, like a constrictor viper. Vipers, asps, snakes. Where the Hell is Saint Paddy when ya need 'im?

CATHERINE
This is a delusion, darlin'. You're hallucinatin'. You've got ta sleep.

JOHN
Oh Lard, there's blood. See it streamin' down like long, hot strands of Coney Island taffy? It'll ruin the floorboards, Catherine, if we don't cut her down.

CATHERINE
I promise ya, there's nothin' there! Now, put down that bloody thing before ya cut yourself and come with me!

JOHN

Catherine, look at her eyes. She's starin' straight at me. Like *I* did it. Like *I* was the one hung her. *(He now focuses on Catherine.)* It wasn't me. It was Ireland. And Ireland was right ta do it. Ya killed your husband.

CATHERINE

What did you say? Why are you speakin' this way?

JOHN

'Cause ya killed me with a hatchet right here in my own home. Ya took that blade and with all your might, planted it into my forehead.

CATHERINE

You've gone completely mad.

JOHN

Why did ya do that, Annie?

CATHERINE

I'm not Annie. I'm Catherine, your wife!

JOHN

Why did ya want ta kill me? Are ya fucking someone else? Who is it? Is it Jesse Purdy? Do ya want me out of the way?

CATHERINE

John, you've got ta wake up! You're confused!

JOHN

Who are ya fucking?

CATHERINE

I'll not endure this foulness anymore. Do whatever ya want. Cut the body down, drag it into the woods. Set it on fire and then drink your Guiness into oblivion. But don't accuse me!
Put down the scythe.

JOHN

Put down the scythe? Now, you know I can't do that, Catherine. Not until I've used it proper. Every tool for its purpose.

CATHERINE

What do ya mean?

JOHN

I think ya know what I mean.

CATHERINE

Now, John, I've just called Father Fitz. He'll be here any minute now. You don't want ta do this.

JOHN

I have ta stop ya from killin' me, Annie.

CATHERINE

Listen ta me. And listen well. I am Catherine Moynahan. Your wife. I am not Annie Walsh. Do ya know how I can prove that? Look up there. See? You're the one showed me. Her body's swingin' from the ceiling.

(Pause)

JOHN

Yes, she is.

CATHERINE
I'm Catherine.

JOHN
And I'm John. *(Pause)* It's a pleasure ta make your acquaintance.

CATHERINE
Now, let's get ya ta bed.

JOHN
But I'm afraid.

CATHERINE
I know. I am too.

JOHN
I can't go ta bed, knowing Annie Walsh is still hangin' here, waitin' for me.

CATHERINE
You can cut her down.

JOHN
I can't. I'm too scared. Dead bodies frighten me. If I get too close to her corpse, she'll awaken and drag me ta Hell.

CATHERINE
I'll do it, then. I'll cut her down. Now, just give me the scythe. Hand it over, love. Just let me take it and I'll make her go away. *(She very carefully pulls the scythe from John's hand. He lets go.)* That's it. That's a good boy.

JOHN

At the rope just above the noose. Cut there. That'll bring the body down. It'll drop to the floor and then we can drag it out and set the bloody thing afire.

(Catherine reaches upward with the blade and mimes cutting the rope. Then watching the body drop to the floor.)

CATHERINE

There. She's down now. See? See, Love? She can't hurt us anymore.

JOHN

I dreamt that you wanted ta kill me in my sleep. So that you could be with Jesse Purdy. I dreamt that Jesse tried ta poison me with insecticide. In a glass of milk.

CATHERINE

An absolute nightmare, Darlin'. Jesse is your best friend in the world. Why would he want to hurt you?

JOHN

We had a Donny-brook over somethin' he found under the house.

CATHERINE

It's over now. It's time we called a doctor ta come and look at ya.

JOHN

I'm afraid of Annie Walsh. I don't want her
hangin' in our living room anymore.

CATHERINE

I agree. Her rotting corpse clashes with the carpet. We'll do whatever we have ta. We'll call a good doctor. And Father Fitz will be here shortly ta help ya. I've asked him ta deliver you Eucharist. He'll bless the house again, as well.

JOHN

What if I toss and turn in my sleep? I'll keep ya up all night.

CATHERINE

You go up ta kip alone. I'll bed down with the children. And I'll check on ya in the mornin'.

JOHN

Catherine,...

CATHERINE

Yes?

JOHN

There's only one thing I know for certain anymore.

CATHERINE

What's that, Love?

JOHN

I'm goin' ta die in this house very soon.

(A change in the tone of underscoring music. It is a sad piano. With tears in her eyes, Catherine kisses John's overheated forehead and gestures for him to go to the sofa. As he does so, she helps him. Once there, she fluffs a pillow for him and covers him with a throw. Enter Eileen. She addresses the audience.)

EILEEN

Mother took Da up to their bed. He hardly had the strength ta make the journey to their bedroom. He was clearly runnin' a fever by now.

(Catherine feels his forehead. She then helps him into bed and tucks him in.)

Ma treated his ailment with tried and true Irish home remedies…

(Catherine returns to John's 'bedside' with a small tray of items.)

A hot glass of Jameson Whiskey from County Cork. She stirred in some sour lemon, fresh cloves, and salted honey.

(Catherine lifts his head to help him drink.)

His chaser was a spoonful of Buckfast. A sweet wine thick as corn syrup.
(Catherine gets him to swallow the dose of Buckfast.)

Finally, she rubbed together a stalk of Dock leaves. These Dock leaves, it is said, cools the flesh. The sap, when applied to the skin, has great healing properties. Suddenly, the stillness in the bedroom was shattered by the pounding of what seemed an unholy entity at the front door.

[End of Scene]

Scene 8

"Mortal Coil"

(Music bleeds in from previous scene. Suddenly, an immediate and ungodly loud pounding at the front door. It is rhythmic and threatening in tone. Eileen runs off to the bedroom hallway in fear. Catherine, startled, runs to the door. She puts her ear to the jam before unlocking.)

CATHERINE
Who is it?! What do ya want?

(No answer. The pounding begins again. This time more threatening.)

CATHERINE
Who are ya?! I'll ring the police, I will!

FATHER FITZGERALD
It's ok! It's Garrett Fitzgerald, Mrs. Moynahan!

(Catherine unlocks, then opens the door to let him in. He has his leather communion kit. The sound of wind blowing can be heard. Any foliage visible outside the door sways in the gusts.)

CATHERINE
Oh, thank God it's you. Come in outta the cold!

FATHER FITZGERALD
I got here as quickly as I could.

CATHERINE

It's fine. The knockin' frightened me, I have ta tell ya.

FATHER FITZGERALD

Terribly sorry about that. Ya see the wind has picked up somethin' terrible outside. I was afraid no one would hear me.

CATHERINE

It's ok. I think all of Long Island heard ya.

FATHER FITZGERALD

Again, my apologies if I startled ya in any way.

CATHERINE

It's all right, Father. You're here now. John's upstairs in bed. He just had some sort of hallucination.

FATHER FITZGERALD

Has he a fever?

CATHERINE

Not certain. Head felt hot when I kissed him.
I'll ring a doctor in the morn.

FATHER FITZGERALD

He must take the body and blood of Christ. I'll go up now.

CATHERINE

He says he thinks he's goin' ta die.

FATHER FITZGERALD
Not on my watch.

CATHERINE
This house'll kill us all, given a chance. Ya know that.

FATHER FITZGERALD
Well, we'll just see that we don't give it a chance, won't we? No, Mrs. Moynahan. Don't give up hope. I'll do all I can ta help. But I must start now. I advise ya get some rest.

CATHERINE
Thank you. I'll rest. I'll be sleepin' with
Marguarite tonight… And Father?

FATHER FITZGERALD
Yes?

CATHERINE
God bless ya. She kisses him on the cheek.

FATHER FITZGERALD
I'll go up now.

(Mysterious music in to underscore the following. Garrett nods to Catherine, she exits. He crosses himself and begins a slow yet deliberate climbing of the stars to John's bedroom.

The priest, at John's beside makes the sign of the cross over John. He throws holy water over John and around the bed. He turns his back to the audience, places his leather kit on the bedside table and removes a ceremonial grail, a small vial of wine, and a velvet bag with holy wafers.

John awakes, turns to face Father Fitzgerald and for a moment the audience cannot see what Garrett is doing with his hands. John can see, however. The priest pours wine into the goblet, and takes a wafer from the bag. Nothing should look out of the ordinary. But this moment should be hidden from the view of the audience. Garrett then sits on the side of John's bed.

Lightning flashes outside the quarter moon windows. Father Fitzgerald gently helps to hold John's head up as he places the wafer on his tongue. The priest mouths words that cannot be heard by the audience. He then places the grail to John's lips and has him take a swallow of wine.

Garrett then appears to make the sign of the cross on John's forehead and lays him back down to sleep. The priest tucks him in, takes John's hands in his own and says a silent prayer. He grabs his kit and places his things back inside. He descends the stairs and exits by the front door. The moment Father Fitzgerald closes the front door behind him, slowly, the kitchen side door begins to open seemingly by itself. Fog drifts in from outside over the threshold and then across the kitchen floor.

In steps Jesse Purdy. He has a strange look on his face as if under hypnosis. Trance-like, he enters the kitchen, leaving the door open behind him and fog continues to creep in floating upon an odd green, haunting light.

Purdy is dressed in long-johns only, as if he'd just gotten out of bed. He carries in the large labeled container of Hydrogen Cyanide. He glides dreamlike up the stairs, still in his trance. He goes into John's bedroom.

John is still conscious, still awake. He cannot speak. He merely looks at Jesse in surprise. Jesse turns his back to the audience as he places the pesticide on the bedside table. The audience cannot see what he is doing with this hands but he is pouring something into another vessel.

Though the pitcher of milk is on the table, it is implied he may have poured the container of poison into an opaque glass. He reaches over, lifts the head of the weakening John and pours the liquid down John's throat. John swallows, he winces as though tasting something strong and bitter.

Still in his "sleep", Jesse Purdy turns and descends the stairs, leaving his pesticide on the bed-stand. He glides down the stairs and crosses to the kitchen. He exits through the door.

John violently convulses as if having a severe reaction to poisoning. He struggles to sit up. He attempts to scream for help but no sound escapes his lips. He foams at the mouth, soaked in perspiration and appears to start choking from being strangled by unseen hands. He uses all the strength he has left, reaches over to the bedside table, opens a drawer, takes out a pencil and a small sheet of paper.

He gets weaker and weaker still. He has to hold both hands to hold the pencil and move it across the paper chit. He manages to scrawl one sentence, then collapses. His body ends up half off the bed. He goes still. John Moynahan has died. There can be no doubt to the audience that Jesse Purdy has poisoned him. Music continues to play. Lights fade slowly to black. Mysterious, somber nad supernatural music eases in and plays throughout intermission.)

END OF ACT I

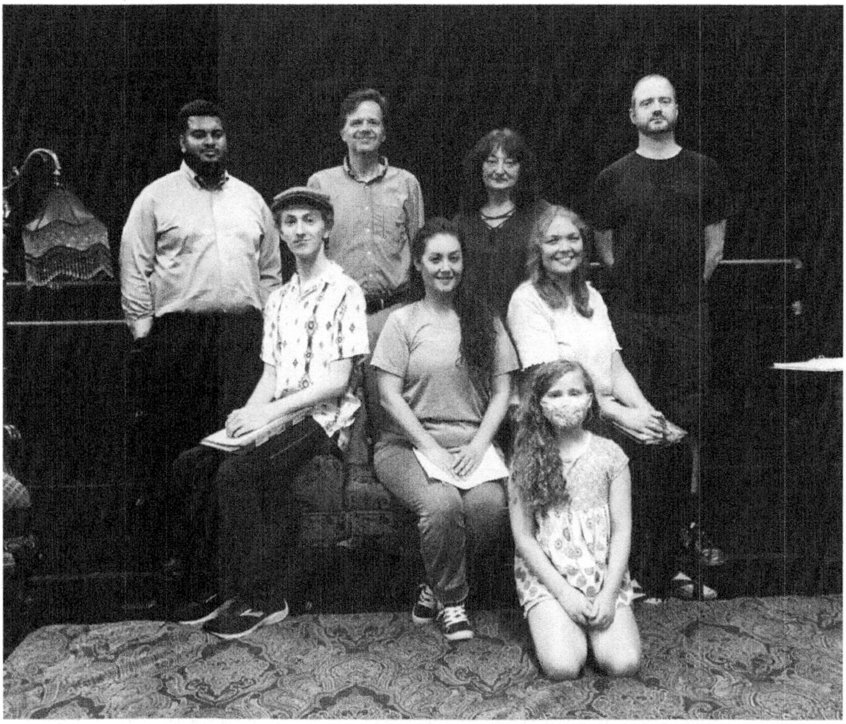

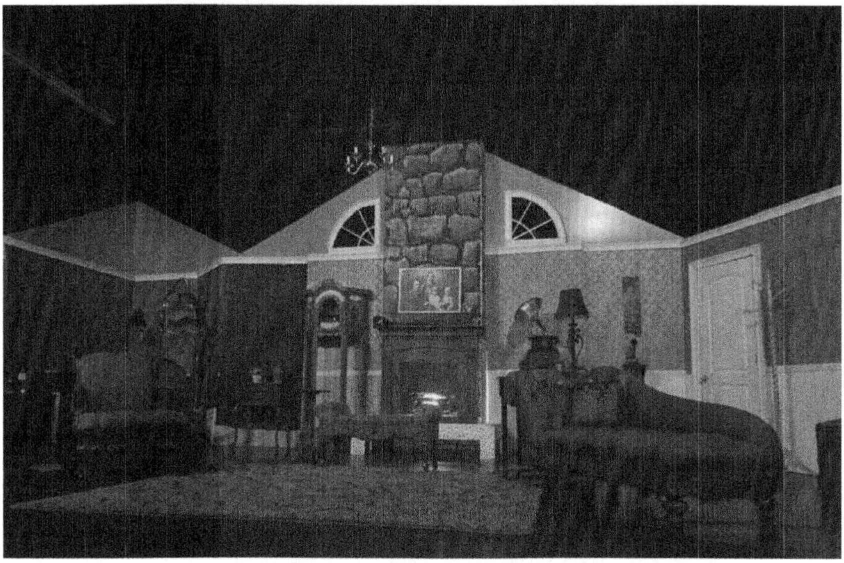

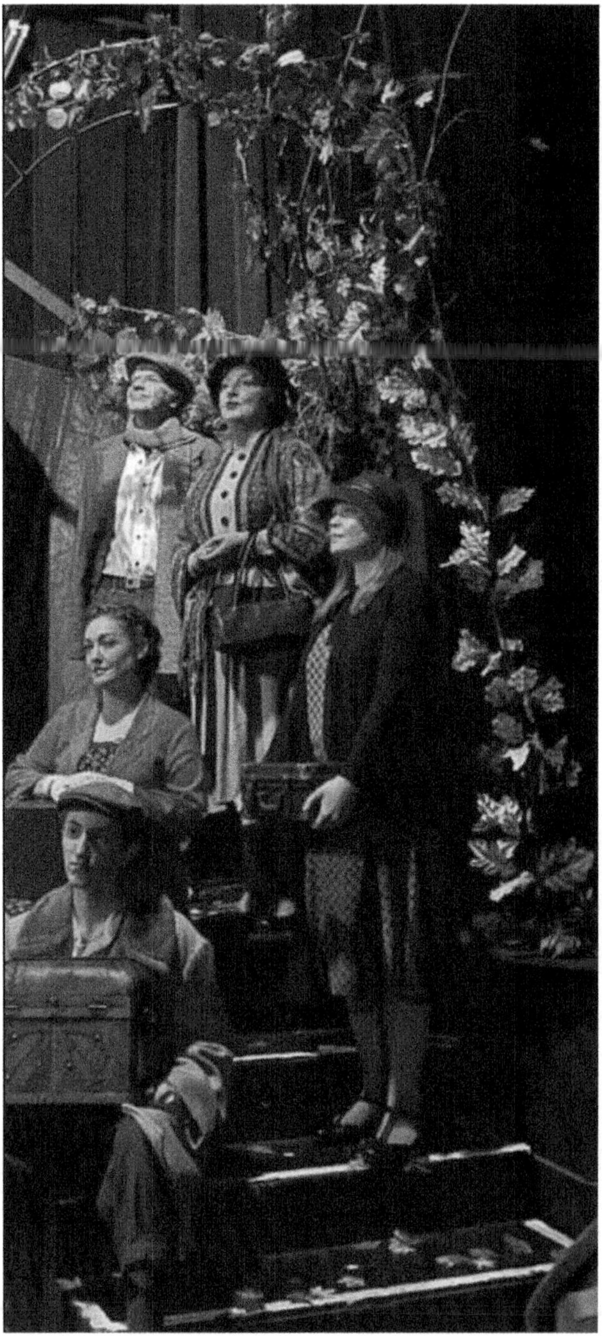

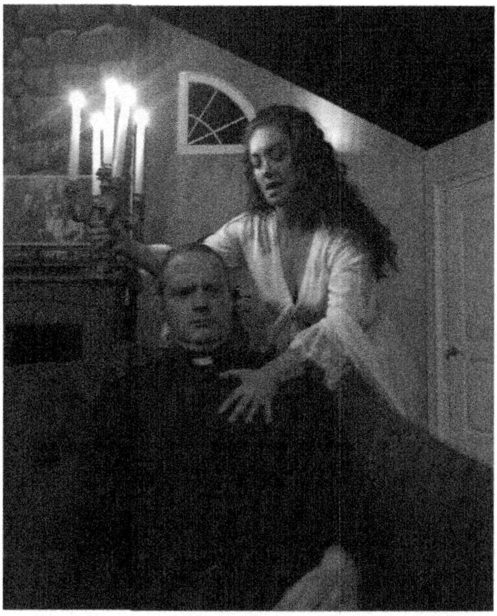

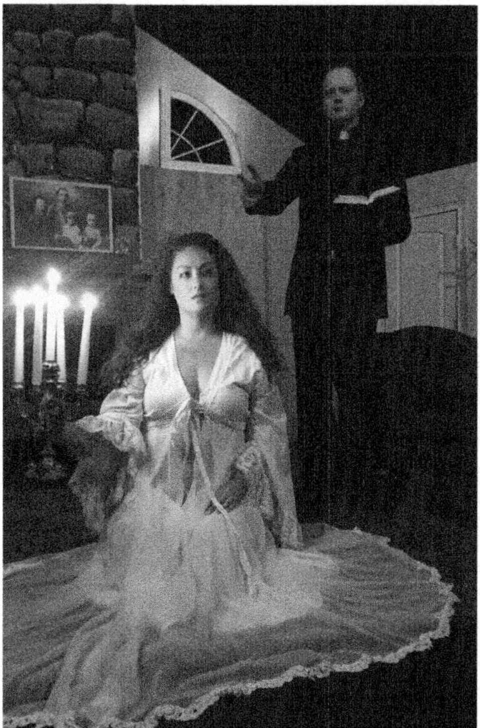

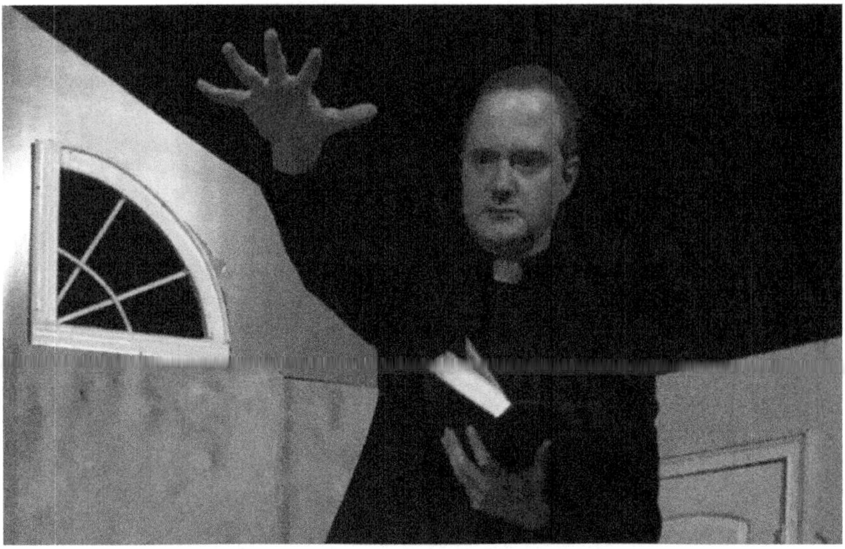

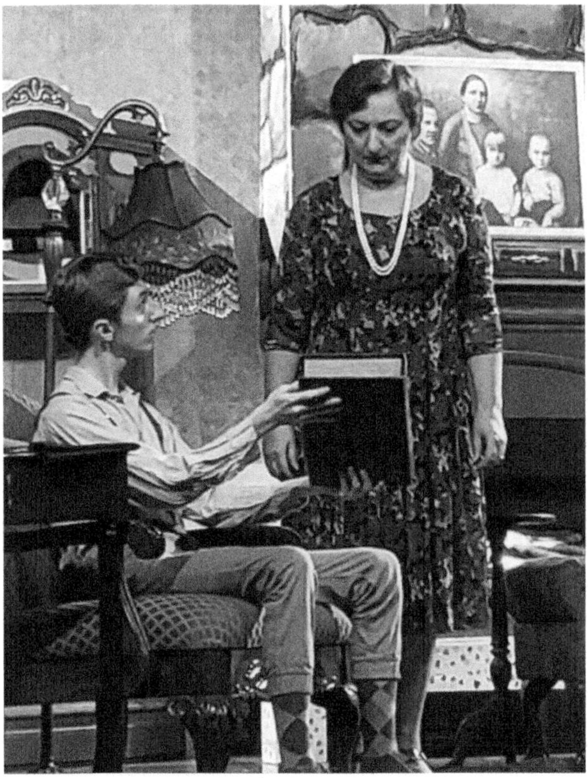

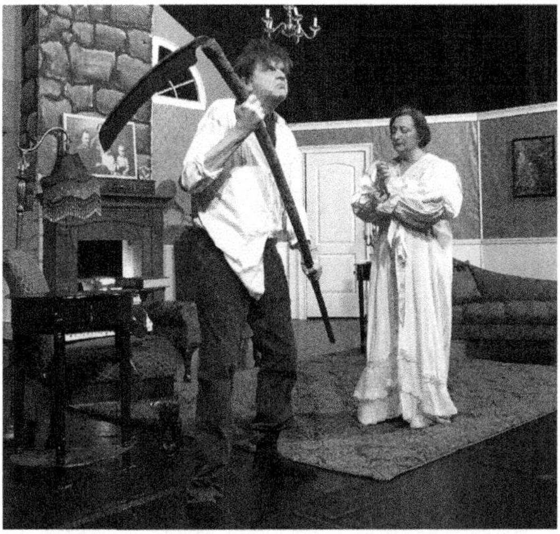

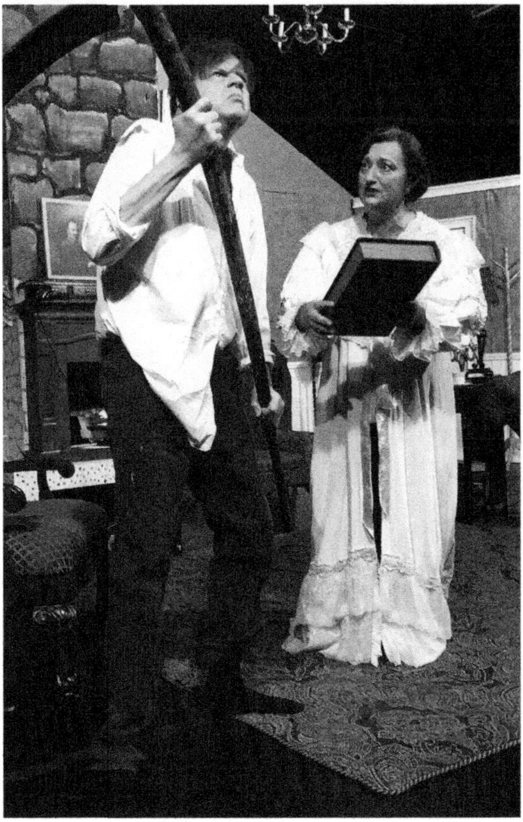

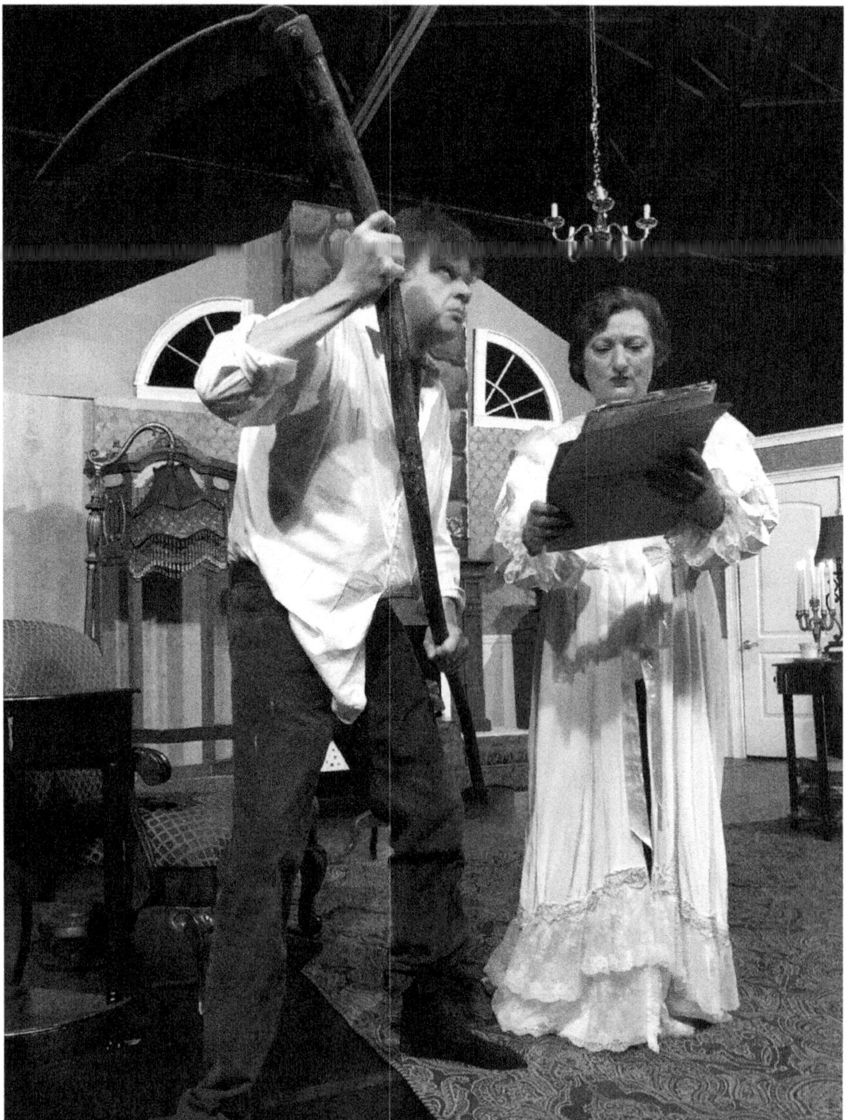

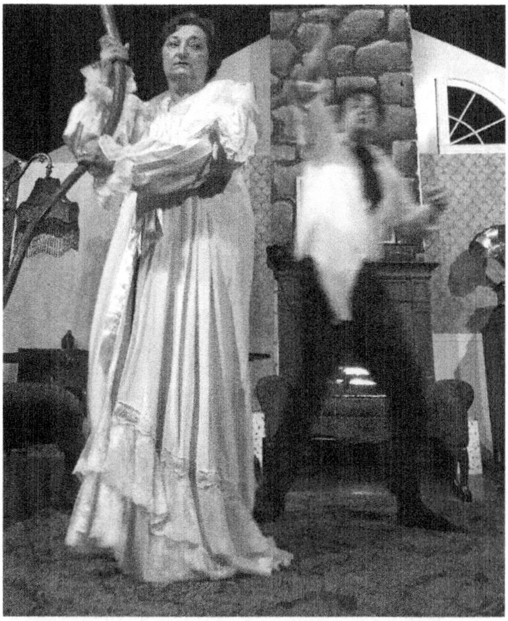

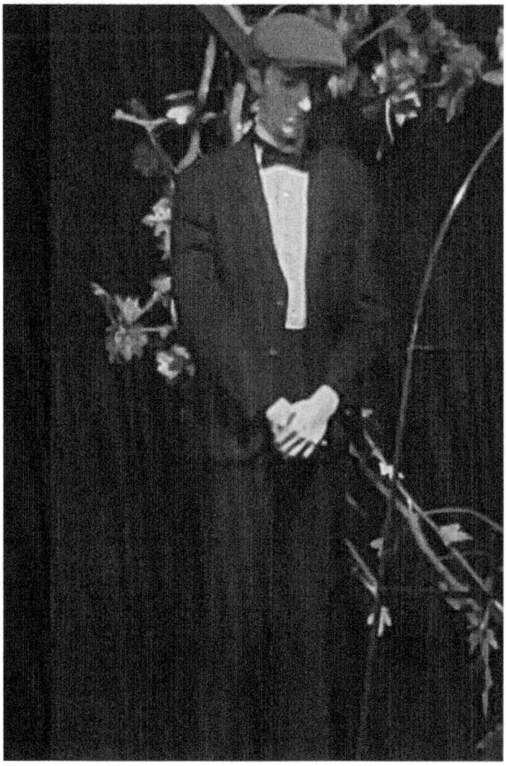

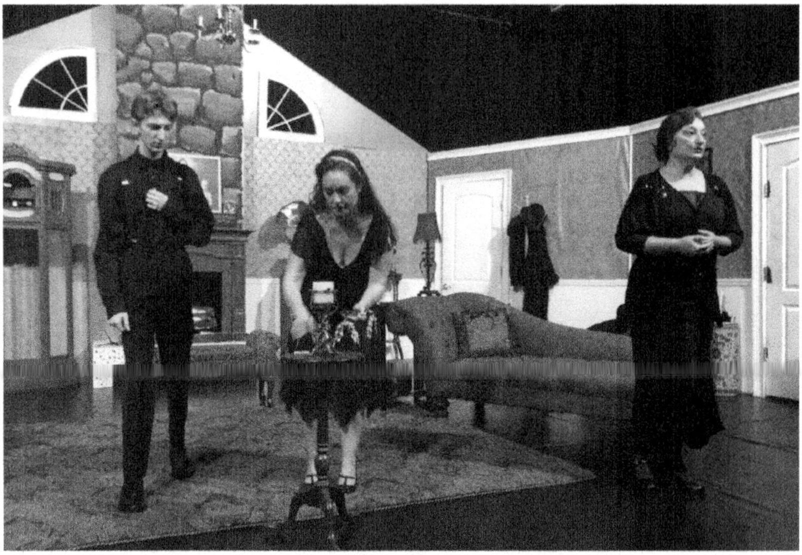

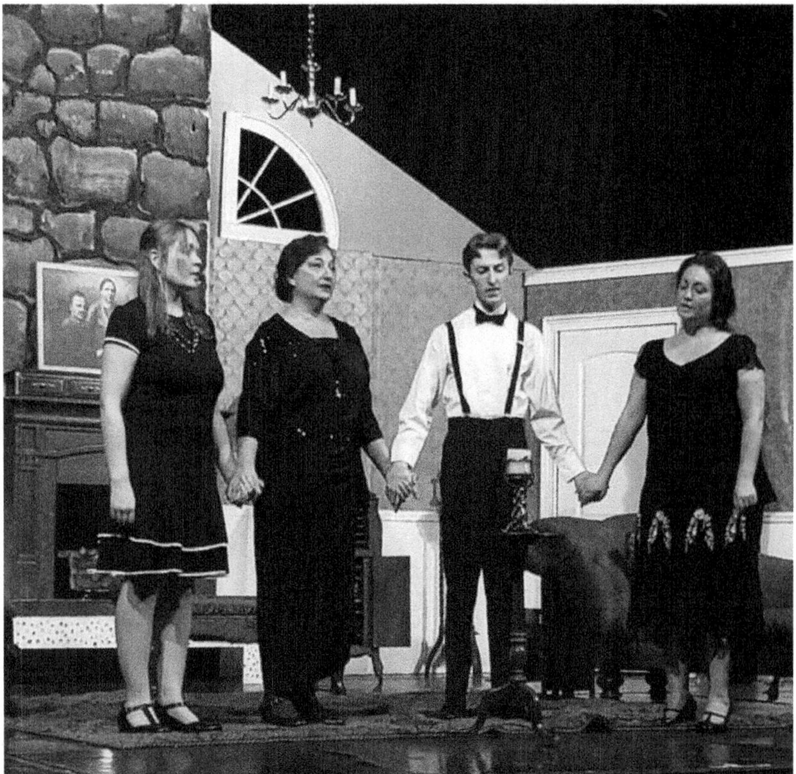

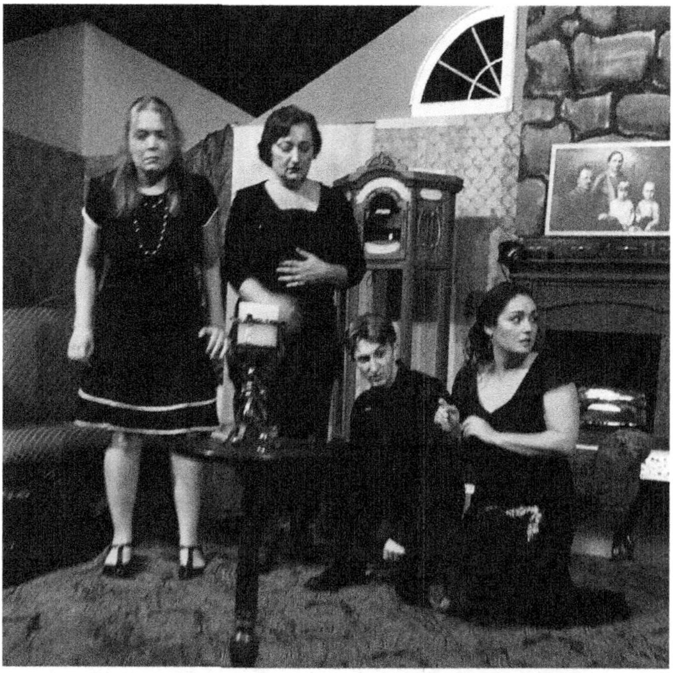

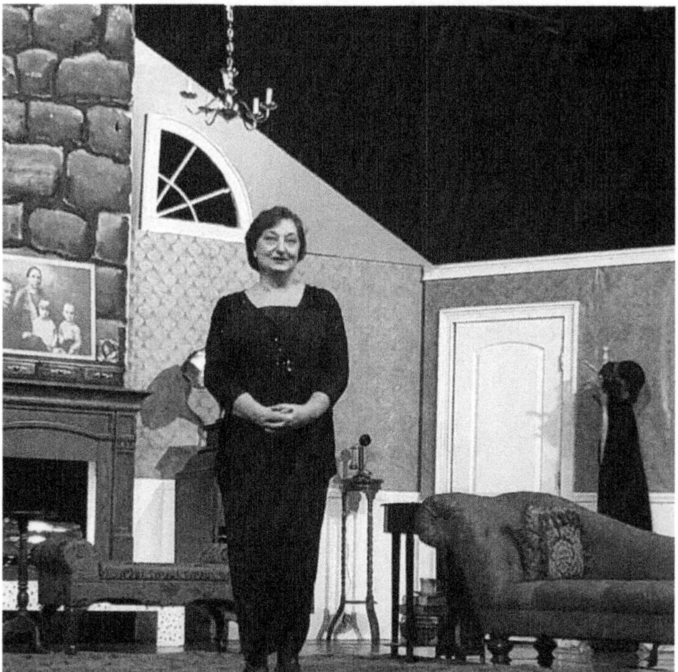

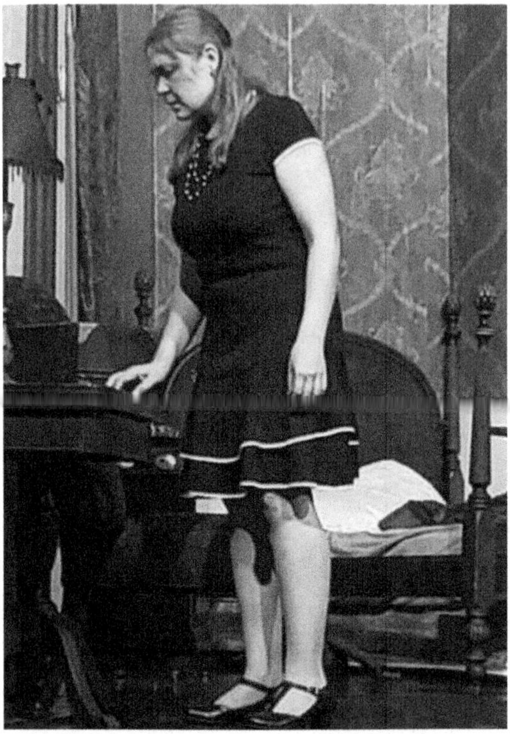

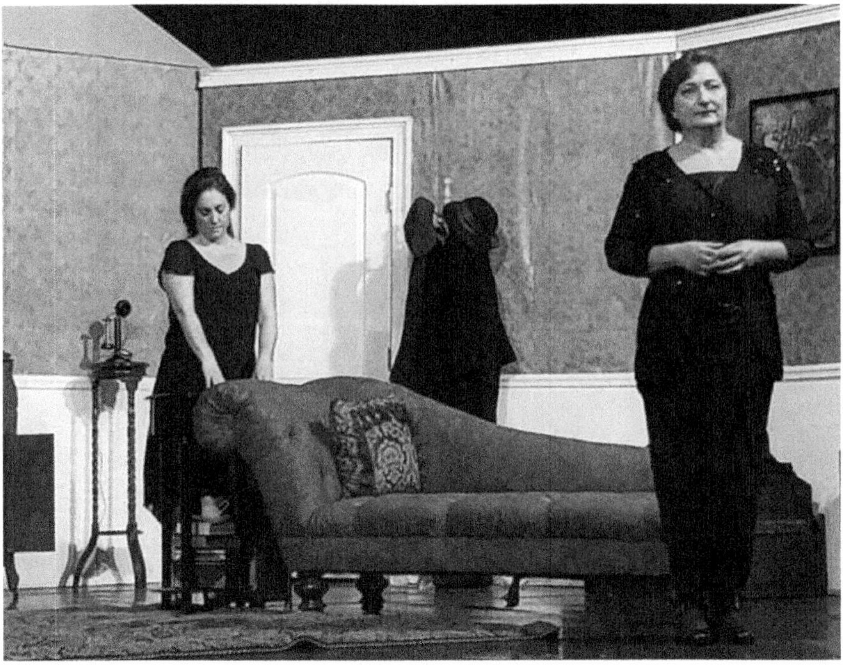

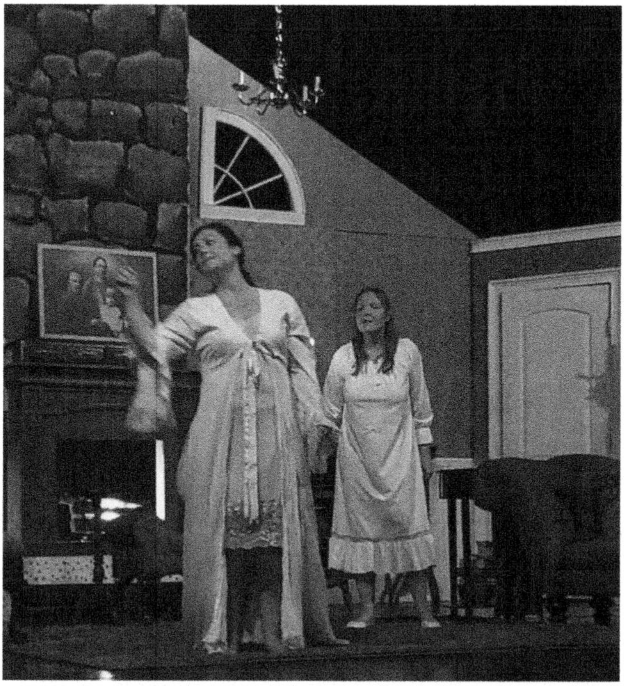

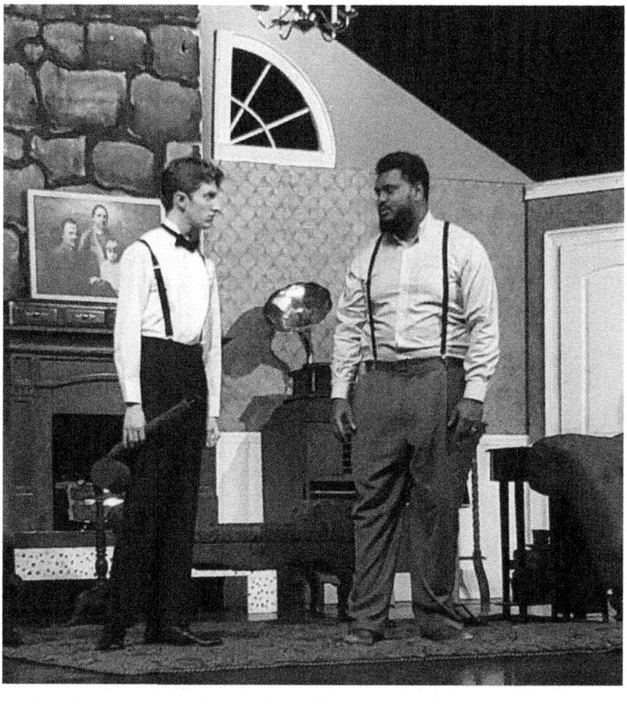

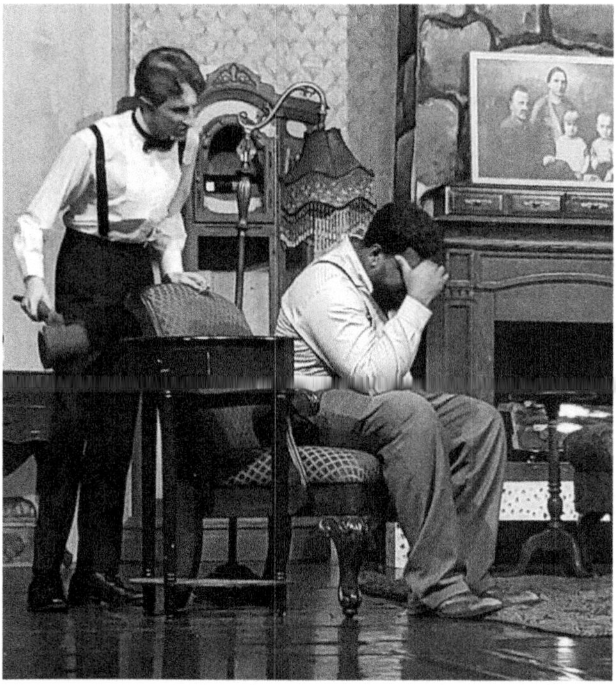

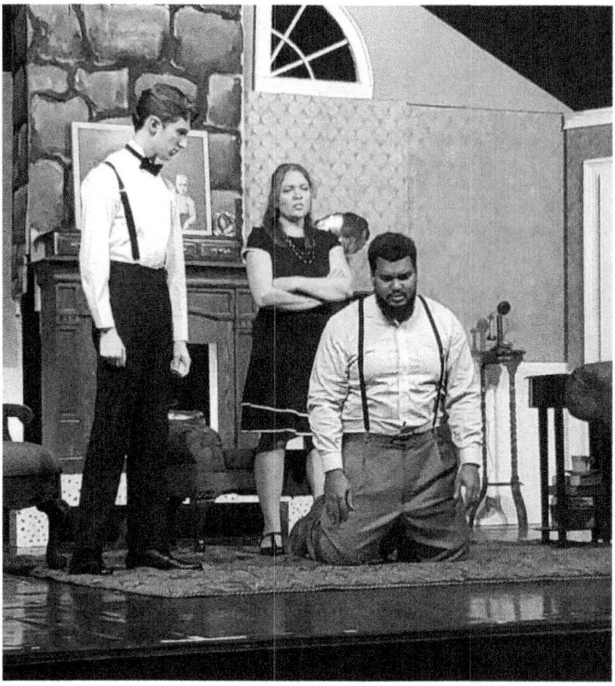

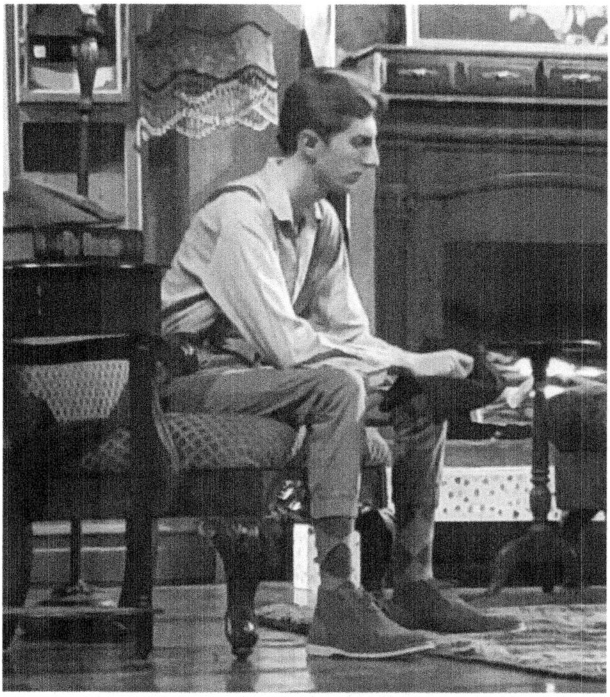

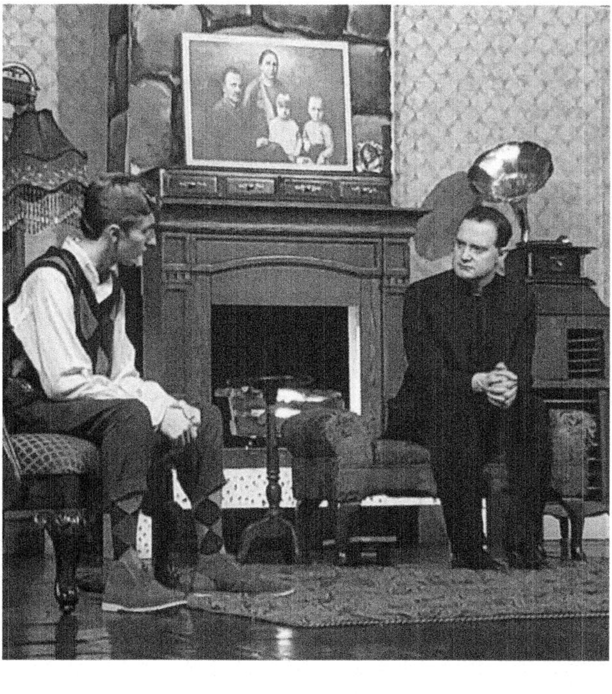

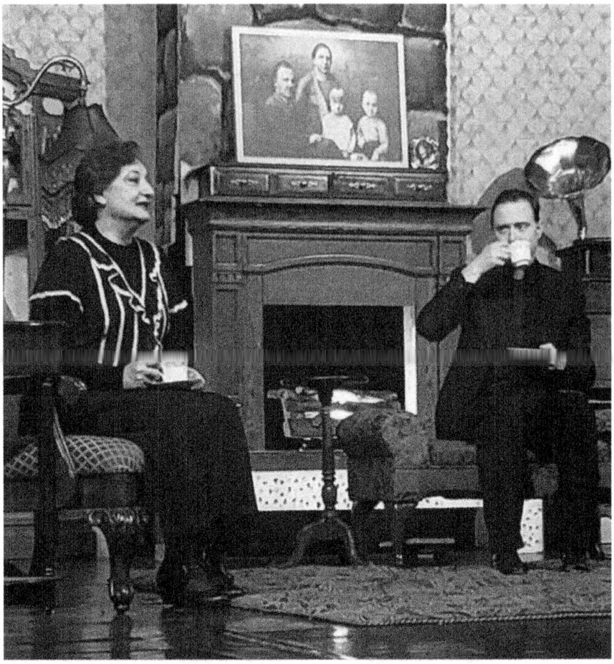

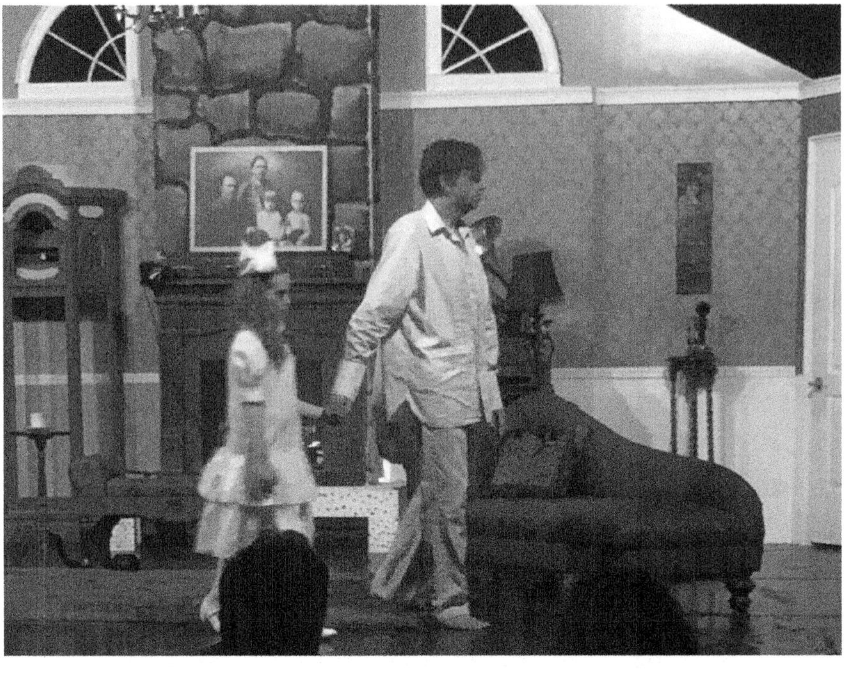

Act II

ACT II

Breakdown of Scenes

Scene 1 "After the Wake" 87
Scene 2 "J'accuse!" 96
Scene 3 "Errand of Mercy" 103
Scene 4 "Making Night Hideous" 113
Scene 5 "Double Exposure" 119
Scene 6 "We Are Resolved" 140

Scene 1

"After the Wake"

(Three days after John Moynahan's death. Lights fade to a darker, bluish hue. It is raining gently. Outside the quarter moon windows above and square windows below, lightning flashes. Thunder. The music is somber, mysterious, moving, and plays throughout the following; It is after the wake. Our attention shifts away from the interior of the home and to what is ostensibly 'outdoors' in the driveway. From the back of the theater house a slow, solemn, funeral procession enters in single file. It is Father Fitzgerald followed by Catherine, followed by Eileen, followed by Marguerite, followed by Thomas, followed by Jesse Purdy. They are each holding up vintage, ornate monochromatic umbrellas. All are wearing the traditional mourning black. They walk slowly, gradually making their way through an aisle toward the stage. As they arrive at the stoop, Father Fitzgerald tacks a letter upon the door. He and Jesse Purdy then peel off from the others and exit Stage Left. Catherine unlocks the door and enters with her three children. All fold their umbrellas and place them in the milk can. They remove hats and coats and hang them in their proper place. Catherine takes a candle from a shelf and places it center on a table without lighting it yet. Eileen sets a plate of Irish wake cakes on another table. Marguerite places a tray of wake cookies in the living room as well. The surviving family members gather in a semi-circle around the table. As music continues to gently underscore, they join hands and recite the following Irish funeral blessing in unison…)

<u>ALL</u>
May those who love us, love us;
and those who don't love us,
May God turn their hearts;
and if he doesn't turn their hearts,
may he turn their ankles
so we'll know them by their limping.

Until we meet again,
may God hold you
in the palm of his hand.
May joy and peace surround you,
contentment latch your door,
and happiness be with you now,
and bless you evermore.

(At this moment they all cross themselves in traditional Catholic fashion. Suddenly, a flame appears on the candle upon the table. Music turns to a darker mood. The family slowly backs away from the table cautiously as they sense a change come over the house. The music bursts into a jump-scare. An immediate explosion of paranormal activity, as the window curtains billow upward, chairs slide across the floor, a few cabinet doors start to slam, books fly across the room, the chandelier swings and sconce lights flicker. The music reaches a fever pitch then just as the family huddles quickly on the floor at center, and a couple of children scream, Catherine cries out a command...)

CATHERINE
In the name of all that is holy, STOP!

(Just as suddenly as the terror began, it all stops immediately. There is quiet. The four gradually look up and out from their huddle. Silence.)

EILEEN
Well,... that was new.

MARGUERITE
Was it somethin' we said?

THOMAS
Whatever it is, it doesn't fancy our furniture arrangement.

~ AMITYVILLE 1925 ~

(As the three younger ones begin straightening the living room and restoring all that has been tossed about, Catherine steps downstage and addresses the audience.)

CATHERINE

The house was angry. After the wake, the supernatural energies had intensified, and they were malevolent. Three days ago my beloved husband John died in our home. The mysterious illness that befell him only days before, had become acute. We found him on the floor just inside the water closet door frame. The coroner said he appeared to have been poisoned by a chemical used in common pesticides.

(Thomas grabs a mop, Eileen a pail, Marguerite a couple of dust cloths. The three slowly, gradually make their way up the stairs.)

With more questions than answers, we decided it was time to cleanse the area of his death bed. I'd been sleepin' on the chaise and refused to enter our bedroom until my children could all go with me. It wasn't long before we found something there. Sometimes the dead leave traces behind. And use the house to whisper clues to fatal diseases, accidents, sudden natural causes… even murder.

(In somber music Catherine joins her children and makes her way up the stairs to the bedroom she shared with John. As Thomas goes onto the floor to pick up used tissues and tea bags, Marguerite clears off the bedside table of tea cups, medicine bottles and water glasses. Catherine and Eileen work together to clear the bed and remake it with fresh linen. Thomas finds Jesse Purdy's pesticide equipment on the bedside table.)

THOMAS
What's Mr. Purdy's equipment doin' up here?

CATHERINE
What's all that?

THOMAS
Looks like his bug poison and pump sprayer.

(Eileen finds a chit of paper under her father's pillow. She pulls it out and reads it silently.)

EILEEN
Ma, look at this.

CATHERINE
What is it, Love?

EILEEN
Some sort of chit. There's writin' on it.

MARGUERITE
Where'd you find it?

EILEEN
Right here under Da's pillow.

THOMAS
What's it say?

MARGUERITE
It's Da's handwritin'.

CATHERINE
Read it aloud.

EILEEN
It appears to say… "The colored man… poisoned… his host".

CATHERINE
Let me see it. (*Reading*) 'The colored man poisoned his host'.

MARGUERITE
Oh dear Lord.

CATHERINE
Your Da must've scribbled this down as he was dyin'.

EILEEN
He was tryin' to tell us what happened. And who killed him.

CATHERINE
Mr. Purdy.

EILEEN
No.

THOMAS
It's all here, his murder weapons and a note from his victim. The deceitful bastard.

CATHERINE
Thomas.

MARGUERITE
Why'd he do it?

THOMAS

We have ta confront him. Now.

CATHERINE

Wait a moment. He told us at the wake that
he'd been sleep-walkin' lately.

THOMAS

So?

EILEEN

It's not possible.

THOMAS

Possible? Anythin' is possible. He did it.

CATHERINE

We need ta make absolute certain he was conscious,
in his right mind, before we go accusin'.

THOMAS

In his right mind? What difference does that make? Ma, what more proof do we need? It's in Da's own hand! Purdy did it, the son of a bitch!

CATHERINE

It just doesn't make sense.

THOMAS

Make sense?! It doesn't have ta make sense!

CATHERINE
Listen ta me, all of you. Before we confront him with this, before we call the authorities, we need to take a breath and not let our anger rule our reason.

MARGUERITE
So how long are we supposed ta wait?

CATHERINE
I need help. I need ta speak with Father Fitzgerald first. He'll know what to do.

EILEEN
Confront Mr. Purdy first. See if he'll confess.

CATHERINE
I can't. I cannot trust myself with my own hands. If I see him, I may just take the law into my own hands. And the bible tells us, 'Vengeance is mine, saith the Lord'. No, I need holy counsel first.

THOMAS
Ma, why is this even a question?! It's clear Purdy killed Da. I'm callin' the police.

MARGUERITE
No, wait!

THOMAS
He's goin' ta jail!

CATHERINE
Thomas, stop!!

THOMAS
No, MA! Let me go!

MARGUERITE
Thomas, listen ta Ma. Let her fetch Father Fitz first.

CATHERINE
We're all goin' together. I'm not going to let my children stay alone one more minute in this house.

EILEEN
Someone needs ta stay here in case the police come askin' questions.

MARGUERITE
And besides we may get visitors from the wake.

THOMAS
They can choke themselves on funeral cakes for all I care.
(Pause)

CATHERINE
All right. the moment I leave, stay outside the door. The three of ya. Now promise me.

EILEEN
All right, Ma.

CATHERINE
I'm off to the rectory. Promise me. You'll leave Jesse alone until I get advice from Father Fitz. Don't call him, don't go ta him. Don't confront him.

EILEEN
We promise.

(Catherine pauses for a moment, grabs her things and exits. Marguerite closes the front door behind her mother. She then turns to Eileen and Thomas.)

MARGUERITE
Go get him, Eileen.

EILEEN
What about you and Thomas?

MARGUERITE
No, you go. He'll listen ta you. I'll stay here with Thomas outside the house.

THOMAS
What'll ya tell him? Ya can't let on that ya know or else he'll never come.

EILEEN
I'll tell him whatever that thing from Hell is down under the house… It's now breakin' up through the floor. That'll get him here.

(Music in. Light change. Eileen exits by the front door to get Jesse. Marguerite and Thomas go the front door stoop steps.)

[End of Scene]

Scene 2

"J'accuse!"

(Later that afternoon. As transition music and a blackout take us into the scene, Eileen, Thomas, and Jesse enter in stage darkness through the front door, and go to the living room center, Jesse lies down on the floor as if he's crumbled from some emotional gut punch. Thomas grabs his father's note, Eileen takes a position of power upstage center, Marguerite sits on the top step outside the front door. All happens throughout Marguerite's following aside to the audience. Lights rise on her.)

MARGUERITE

Eileen went ta fetch Jesse Purdy. She found him later that afternoon. We presented him with our evidence and gave him the third degree. It felt like we'd been at it for hours. Hours on end, questionin' and accusin'. Until the man collapsed upon the floor in tears. His will to live shakin' by the realization that he'd unknowingly murdered his 'Host', our Da. My own sleep-walkin' was called into question. But we had the note, we had his insecticide equipment, and we had his boot prints at the bedside. There would be no escapin' justice for Jesse Purdy.

(Lights rise and Marguerite goes inside to join the other three.)

THOMAS
One last time, Mr. Purdy... What does this note mean?

JESSE
I been telling you. I don't know what else you want me to say.

EILEEN
We want the truth.

JESSE
I don't know what the truth is anymore.

MARGUERITE
Well the only other person who knows what happened is our father. And he can't exactly serve as a material witness.

EILEEN
Ya do realize that the only reason yar not in jail right now is due to our mother's grace.

JESSE
I know that.

MARGUERITE
She couldn't bear ta see your face. She was afraid she might kill ya.

THOMAS
She's off ta find Father Fitzgerald. She wants spiritual guidance ta keep from rippin' ya apart.

EILEEN
How long have ya had this sleep-walkin' problem?

JESSE
It started as soon as I broke ground on this property.

THOMAS
How do ya know that?

JESSE
Because in the mornings I'd find leaves and
dirt in the foot of my bedsheets.

THOMAS
What difference does it make? Da wrote a death
note. It's right here. He named *you*.

EILEEN
The coroner made his findings clear. Da was most probably poisoned from chemicals found in pesticides.

JESSE
How do they think *that* happened?

MARGUERITE
An accident of some kind. Cross-contamination they called it.

THOMAS
But *we* know the truth.

JESSE
Who else knows?

MARGUERITE
We've not told a soul. For now this is a private family matter.

EILEEN
Mr. Purdy… Why? Why did ya do it?

JESSE
I don't know!

THOMAS
That's not good enough!

JESSE
I wouldn't have killed him had I been in my right mind. I'd hang myself before I'd intentionally hurt your father.

MARGUERITE
Mr. Purdy, now,... think real hard. Try ta remember. What happened that night? What do ya recall?

(Music eases in, lights fade to sepia. The ghost of John Moynahan enters from the water closet door upstairs, walks to his and Catherine's bed, and sits. He stares at the proceedings center stage without commenting through facial expression how he feels. He simply watches and listens, stoically. Jesse crosses downstage. Music continues to underscore the following;)

JESSE
Bits and pieces. I know I left my house. I must've thought it was time to spray the shrubs along the front lawn. I remember taking my sprayer and can of pesticide. I don't remember walking inside, though. I put something into a drinking glass. I think I held your father's head back and all I have is a vague recollection of pouring the fluid down his throat… I don't know why I did it. I had no cause to hurt your father.

(Music fades out.)

THOMAS
If his memory is this good, then it means he must've been conscious on some level.

MARGUERITE

No. It doesn't mean a thing. He could very well have been under the influence of whatever demon has infested this place.

THOMAS

But he has *some* memory. So it proves he was aware what he was doin' at the time.

MARGUERITE

A person can recall events even in a blackout, can't they, Eileen?

EILEEN

Like a dream, Thomas. Everyone dreams they are doin' things that they wouldn't otherwise do in their waking life.

MARGUERITE

Were you dreamin', Mr. Purdy?

THOMAS

Or were you awake?

JESSE

You have to believe me, Thomas. It wasn't the real me.

THOMAS

But it was your hands that did it. You're still culpable on some level, Mr. Purdy.

JESSE
I know I never intended to harm your father. I had to have thought I was giving him a glass of water. I must've mistaken my jar of insecticide for the pitcher by his bedside. I thought I was pouring water into his glass.

THOMAS
But it wasn't water. Was it? We found the pesticide on his bedside table. Ya sleep-walked your way into our house. Ya climbed the stairs. Ya went into their bedroom. You filled the drinkin' glass with poison, and Da was too weak ta fight ya. Then you made him drink. He had just enough life left in him to scribble this note.

JESSE
You want I should turn myself in.

MARGUERITE
It would be easier.

JESSE
For whom?

EILEEN
For us… Our mother… Your conscience.

JESSE
I was not awake when I did it. I wasn't myself. So I'm not accountable to the law. I am accountable to God. As Thomas says, it was my hands that ultimately ended your father's life. I know that. My hands killed your father. And for that, I deserve to face persecution by God. I deserve to die at his hands.

THOMAS
If ya really feel that way, Mr. Purdy, I can spare God the trouble.

JESSE
You won't have to, Thomas… You won't have to.

(Jesse exits by the front door. Music in, lights fade to transition into next scene.)

[End of Scene]

Scene 3

"Errand of Mercy"

(Eileen, Marguerite, and Thomas have exited. It is an hour later. Catherine enters from front door. Father Fitzgerald follows her into the living room. Transitional music fades.)

CATHERINE
… No, Father! I've made my decision.

FATHER FITZGERALD
Think it over, Catherine.

CATHERINE
I have.

FATHER FITZGERALD
You have a responsibility to John.

CATHERINE
I also have a responsibility to protect John's good friend. If he *were* sleep-walkin', wouldn't that change things?

FATHER FITZGERALD
Catherine, why did you come to me for advice?

CATHERINE
What do ya mean?

FATHER FITZGERALD

I mean, if ya were already so resolute in your
thoughts, why ask me for mine?

CATHERINE

I don't know. I suppose I thought that if ya agreed with me, I'd feel a lot better about not goin' to the police. At least, not just yet.

FATHER FITZGERALD

My advice still stands. Contact the authorities
with what you've found, or *I* will have ta.

CATHERINE

But *why* do ya have ta?

FATHER FITZGERALD

My office,… my conscience,… my commitment to the holy word.

CATHERINE

And what does the holy word say?

FATHER FITZGERALD

Well, Isaiah said… "Bring justice to the fatherless, and please the widow's cause." And Micah said "What does the Lord require of you but to do justice?"

(Pause)

CATHERINE

Lighten my mood, huh, Father? Tell me somethin' funny.

FATHER FITZGERALD

All right. True story… A Presbyterian once stumbled into my confessional. He had no idea what to do. So, he sat his bum down on the kneeler, paused, and tried the ol' 'Shave and a Haircut' game.

(He demonstrates using a nearby table to pound out the first five knocks.)

KNOCK – KNOCK – KNOCK – KNOCK – KNOCK!

CATHERINE

And what did you do?

FATHER FITZGERALD

I knocked back.

(He wraps out the final two knocks.)

KNOCK – KNOCK!

(A small chuckle, a little smile from both. Pause, as Catherine gets an idea.)

FATHER FITZGERALD

True story.

CATHERINE

Wait! Just a moment…

FATHER FITZGERALD

Yes, Catherine?

CATHERINE

You've just given me an idea.

FATHER FITZGERALD
What is it?

CATHERINE
Please, sit down.

(He sits.)

FATHER FITZGERALD
Go ahead, Catherine.

CATHERINE
It's this… could there possibly be… a loophole of some sort?

FATHER FITZGERALD
A loophole? What do ya mean?

CATHERINE
Well,… suppose for example,… Jesse were to come to you. Not as a friend, but rather in a more clergical nature.

FATHER FITZGERALD
I'm listenin'.

CATHERINE
And suppose he came to ya for confession?

FATHER FITZGERALD
You're suggestin' he confess his crime to me?

CATHERINE
I am.

FATHER FITZGERALD
He's not even Catholic.

CATHERINE
Yes. Lucky him.

FATHER FITZGERALD
Indeed.

CATHERINE
The point is, if he were to confess his transgression to you... If he were truly repentant, and told ya what he did, it would still be considered a confession, even from a protestant.

FATHER FITZGERALD
Technically speaking, yes. But it wouldn't protect him from the law.

CATHERINE
Why not? You would be precluded from goin to the police. You'd be bound to honor your oath of confidentiality.

FATHER FITZGERALD
In theory.

CATHERINE
Your commitment to Clery-Parishioner privilege would have to be maintained. Isn't that right?

FATHER FITZGERALD
In theory, yes, but you see…

CATHERINE
It would solve this conundrum, would it not? It could buy us a little time to decide exactly what to do.

FATHER FITZGERALD
Not exactly. It doesn't work like that.

CATHERINE
Why not?

FATHER FITZGERALD
Because as a citizen, I already have knowledge of his crime. Independent of my office, prior to his steppin' into the confessional.

CATHERINE
So, if you learned of the murder in confession first, you could keep silent about it?

FATHER FITZGERALD
In short, yes.

CATHERINE
What's the difference?

FATHER FITZGERALD
The difference is, it didn't happen that way. *You* told me first. I'm not just a priest, I'm a law-abiding citizen of Amityville.

CATHERINE
But his crime is also the ultimate sin. And it's quite probable that he wasn't in his right mind when he did it. Does he not then deserve absolution as any child of God?

FATHER FITZGERALD
I cannot offer him absolution.

CATHERINE
But you can hear him.

FATHER FITZGERALD
I can. Catherine, I can listen to him. I can allow him to open his heart to me. And I can pray with him.

CATHERINE
Will you go to him? He may be at his home or the Hardware. He's also building another house down the street.

FATHER FITZGERALD
Yes, I'll find him.

CATHERINE
Will you at least consider what we've discussed.

FATHER FITZGERALD
I will. I'll hear his confession, and I'll make a decision after. I'll let you know.

CATHERINE
Thank you. Just consider.

FATHER FITZGERALD
I will.

CATHERINE
Bless you.

(Father Fitzgerald goes to the front door, stops, then turns back.)

FATHER FITZGERALD
Catherine,… just one other thing.

CATHERINE
Yes?

FATHER FITZGERALD
This,… this Agatha Ketchum ya told me about,… the little dead girl,….

CATHERINE
Yes?

FATHER FITZGERALD
If her spirit is indeed here, in this house… She was able to counteract my blessin' the other day.

CATHERINE
Why would her spirit do that?

FATHER FITZGERALD
It means she rejected Christ. Either that or,…

CATHERINE
Or?

FATHER FITZGERALD
It's not her doin' the hauntin', the disturbances.
The curse upon your home.

CATHERINE
What are ya tellin' me?

FATHER FITZGERALD
This may be somethin' far more malevolent.
Somethin' positively dangerous.

CATHERINE
Like what, for God's sake?

FATHER FITZGERALD
Oh, it isn't for God's sake. It may be Lucifer himself.

CATHERINE
God help us!

FATHER FITZGERALD
He will. And *I* will.

CATHERINE
Bless you. Now, please,... Go find Mr. Purdy.

FATHER FITZGERALD
I will. And I'll save this family. Ya have my word.

(Catherine opens the door for him and he exits. Just as he is on the stoop at the bottom of the steps, she stops him.)

CATHERINE
Oh, Father....

FATHER FITZGERALD
Yes?

CATHERINE
Please tell Father Giovanni he's in our prayers.

FATHER FITZGERALD
I will do that.

(Father Fitzgerald exits. Catherine closes the door, then addresses the audience.)

CATHERINE
I learned something in that conversation with Father Fitz. Later that same day I gathered up Eileen, Marguerite, and Thomas. We talked over everything at dinner that evening. To remind us of happier times in Dublin, we had coddle and colcannon. And though we had misgivings about sleepin' in our separate rooms, we persevered. Exhausted from the day's events, and prolonged discussions on what we should do, we fell fast asleep in our respective rooms. I slept solid. My daughters, not so much.

(In transition music, Catherine ascends the stairs to her bedroom, gets undressed and crawls into bed.)

[End of Scene]

Scene 4

"Making Night Hideous"

(Dim lighting. Wall sconces glow in ghostly fashion. Suddenly, the light on the Victrola comes on. The opening chimes of John McCormick's "Three o'Clock in the Morning" begin ringing once again. As the song plays, low-lying fog creeps in upon the center floor. The ghost of John Moynahan enters from the privy door upstage with scythe in hand. He descends the stairs, dragging the farm scythe blade across the floor behind him. He goes to the Victrola and turns off the song. Immediately blending in with the end of the song is ominous music that plays throughout the scene. John's Ghost goes exits through the kitchen archway.

Marguerite enters from the hall door in a hypnotic state, sleep-walking in her nightgown. She carries a stack of Thomas's photos in her hand. She goes to center of the living room and begins writing in the air with her finger. Her lips are moving as she is reading the words she 'sees' on her father's note in the air. Nothing is heard from her voice, however. Eileen enters from the hall door in her nightgown and carries with her a fully-lit candelabra to light her way. She sees Marguerite and carefully approaches her center.)

<u>EILEEN</u>
Marguerite! What are you doing?

<u>EILEEN</u>
Marguerite!... You're sleep walkin' again. Wake up.

<u>MARGUERITE</u>
Marguerite is in her bedroom. Asleep.

EILEEN
No she isn't. You're standin' right here.

MARGUERITE
I assure you, I am not your sister.

EILEEN
Who are ya then?

MARGUERITE
Agatha. Agatha Ketchum.

EILEEN
All right, Marguerite. I'll play along. Are you the little girl who died on this land?

MARGUERITE
Yes.

EILEEN
Where are ya buried? Is your body nearby?

MARGUERITE
Under this house. I was here first. It's so cold down here. And dark. So very cold and damp.

EILEEN
What have ya done with Marguerite?

MARGUERITE
Marguerite is in her bedroom. Asleep.

EILEEN
Those are Thomas' photographs from the day the house was blessed.

MARGUERITE
They're all in order.

EILEEN
In order?

MARGUERITE
See for yourself.

(Marguerite drops the photos to the floor. Eileen doesn't pick them up.)

EILEEN
Marguerite,…

MARGUERITE
Agatha.

EILEEN
Agatha… Do ya know why Jesse Purdy killed our father?

MARGUERITE
Thomas will take pictures of Jesse Purdy hangin' from a Sycamore.

EILEEN
What?!

MARGUERITE
Thomas takes such revealing pictures.

EILEEN
Why are ya here? Why do ya haunt us so?

MARGUERITE
To tell ya about my toys.

EILEEN
Your toys? I don't understand.

MARGUERITE
You will soon enough.

EILEEN
All right… Tell me, Agatha. I'm listenin' to ya.

(Eileen sits.)

MARGUERITE
I loved to play with my toys. I had a miniature Trojan horse. With wooden wheels.

EILEEN
What else?

MARGUERITE
I had a little dolly. A Grandma Riding Hood. She had real human teeth. Brown, broken, jagged.

EILEEN
Why are ya tellin' me this?

MARGUERITE
I loved my stuffed animals, too. My favorite was a little lamb. He was my favorite until he tricked me. On day I could feel something hard under his face. There was something solid in his head. So I took a straight razor and I cut him open. I sliced him from ear to ear. I peeled the fur off his skull. Underneath, there was a face staring back at me. The eyes, the tongue, the horns of Satan himself.

EILEEN
You shouldn't be here.

MARGUERITE
This house has been made unclean.

EILEEN
How?

EILEEN
Ya said Thomas will take photos of Jesse hangin' from a tree. What does that mean?

MARGUERITE
Look at the photos.

EILEEN
Why will he take pictures of that?

MARGUERITE
It's in the photos.

EILEEN
What is?

MARGUERITE
The answer.

EILEEN
Is this how we will discover why Jesse killed our Da?

MARGUERITE
"Believe not the false facades
Of witches and male witchers –
Their truths shall be revealed to you
Look close, their final pictures.

(In a hypnotic state, Marguerite exits back into the hallway door. Eileen crosses downstage to address the audience.)

EILEEN
The next mornin' Marguerite was feelin' herself again. She had little memory of having channeled the spirit of Agatha, but she remembered word for word the rhymin' verse she'd spoken. That same afternoon our family worked to piece together the sad and strange events of the past fortnight. We had new questions and we wanted answers. So, we called upon the help of a friend… I found Father Fitzgerald at the library. I asked him to bless the house again, and to commiserate with us over tragic news I'd delivered to him there;… the unfortunate suicide of our friend… and our father's murderer, Mr. Jesse Purdy.

(Somber music continues. Eileen picks the photos up off the floor. She places them on a back table. She goes to the bedroom hallway door and exits.)

[End of Scene]

Scene 5

"Double Exposure"

(Late afternoon. Marguerite is on the telephone. James is organizing his photos. Eileen is knitting. The doorbell rings and Catherine enters from the kitchen arch to answer it. She is wiping her hands with a dish towel from having been cleaning. At the door is Father Fitzgerald with holy blessing kit in hand. Music fades as Catherine opens the door.)

CATHERINE
Oh, Father Fitzgerald. Good to see you. Please come in.

FATHER FITZGERALD
Thank you.

CATHERINE
Bless ya for comin' over.

FATHER FITZGERALD
Of course. Anything to help.

CATHERINE
May I take your coat?

FATHER FITZGERALD
Please.

CATHERINE
Take off your gloves and stay. We're havin' a difficult time of it today as you can well imagine.

FATHER FITZGERALD
Oh, Catherine, I'm so sorry. Eileen told me the news.

CATHERINE
Tragic. I feel so conflicted.

FATHER FITZGERALD
I know this isn't how ya wanted things to unfold.

CATHERINE
Not at all.

FATHER FITZGERALD
I looked everywhere but I couldn't find him. Had I only known the man was suicidal,…

CATHERINE
Ya couldn't have known. His poor heart was broken knowin' that he'd killed his friend.

FATHER FITZGERALD
I'd made the decision to hear his confession, too. And I had decided that I would honor my vow of confidentiality. Even though these were extreme circumstances.

CATHERINE
Well, I appreciate that you would do that.

FATHER FITZGERALD

So, Eileen asked me to come over and bless the house again.

CATHERINE

Yes, again thank you for comin'. Can I get ya a cup of tea?

FATHER FITZGERALD

That would be wonderful, thank you.

CATHERINE

I'll only be a minute.

(Catherine exits to the kitchen. Marguerite steps away from the telephone table.)

FATHER FITZGERALD

Marguerite.

MARGUERITE

Oh, Father Fitz. Thank ya for comin' over.

FATHER FITZ

Of course. How are ya feelin'? Sleep-walkin' still disturbin' ya?

MARGUERITE

Still, yes…

FATHER FITZGERALD

A pleasure to see you again, Marguerite…. Nice to see you,… uh, fully-dressed, I suppose.

MARGUERITE
Isn't it just horrible about Mr. Purdy?

FATHER FITZGERALD
I'm so sorry. Eileen told me at the library. But I never asked her how you all found out.

MARGUERITE
Thomas heard first.

THOMAS
There was a rumor of a man hangin' from a branch in the woods nearby. I suspected who it may have been. I found him. I had my camera. And I took photos of Mr. Purdy up in a sycamore tree. I developed the pictures as soon as I got back from the precinct. It's not pretty, but I wanted to show them to you. I thought maybe you could say a prayer over them or a blessin' or somethin'.

(Thomas hands the photos to Father Fitzgerald. The priest looks at them and is clearly disgusted.)

FATHER FITZGERALD
Oh good Lord. Mr. Purdy. These are… most upsettin'… to say the least.

MARGUERITE
I can't even look at them. They turn my stomach.

FATHER FITZGERALD
Thomas, perhaps these are better out of the house.

THOMAS
I'm gonna toss them in the rubbish. I just wanted ta show you first.

FATHER FITZGERALD
I understand.

(Father Fitz places his hand on the photos as if to bless them. He hands them back to Thomas. Catherine enters with a cup of tea from the kitchen. She brings it to Father Fitzgerald.)

CATHERINE
Here you are.

FATHER FITZGERALD
Thank you, Catherine.

CATHERINE
My poor John. We miss him so. I wish he were here to make things better. He always had a way of makin' us feel like everythin' would work out all right. And he'd always know just what to say. Even when he'd get things wrong, sometimes. *(Pause)* Why didn't ya correct him?

(Pause)

FATHER FITZGERALD
I'm sorry?

CATHERINE
Why didn't ya correct him?

FATHER FITZGERALD
Is that for me?

CATHERINE
Yes. Why didn't ya correct him?

FATHER FITZGERALD
I don't understand. Correct whom? To whom are you referrin'?

CATHERINE
John.

FATHER FITZGERALD
I'm not sure I follow.

CATHERINE
You see,… my husband always had this annoyin' habit of callin' people by the wrong name. Did it all the time. I'd correct him time and time again, but he couldn't remember names to save his soul. T'was often a point of embarrassment. But it was habitual, so after a while I just stopped helpin' him out.

FATHER FITZGERALD
Catherine,… *(He puts down his cup of tea)* What's this about?

CATHERINE
It's about the other day when ya came over to bless the house.

FATHER FITZGERALD
What about it?

CATHERINE
John asked ya about Father Giovanni.

FATHER FITZGERALD
Yes, I remember.

CATHERINE
He wanted to know about his lumbago.

FATHER FITZGERALD
And I told him that he would be fine. He was in good hands.

CATHERINE
And then, John mentioned him a second time, by name, Father Giovanni.

FATHER FITZGERALD
Yes, I remember.

CATHERINE
I thought ya would. But that's not his name, ya see.

FATHER FITZGERALD
Isn't it?

CATHERINE
No. Ya see? The man's name is Guiseppe. Father Guiseppe, not Giovanni. And ya never corrected him.

FATHER FITZGERALD
What are ya gettin' at?

CATHERINE
Why didn't ya just say, "Oh, Mr. Moynahan, you must be referrin' to Father Guiseppe"?

FATHER FITZGERALD
I,… I probably didn't hear him well. A mistake anyone can make.

CATHERINE
Oh ya heard him. He misspoke twice and ya never caught the error.

FATHER FITZGERALD
Twice, huh?

CATHERINE
And then, yesterday, when ya came over and we discussed you hearin' Mr. Purdy's confession,… ya had all the right answers, all the right bible verses. You were the perfect priest. Almost *too* perfect. You seemed almost rehearsed. I decided to throw ya a test. You were leavin' and I said "Please tell Father Giovanni that we wish him good health". I deliberately misspoke his name. That was the third time ya heard it and the third time ya didn't offer that his true name was Guiseppe. That's when I knew somethin' wasn't quite right about ya.

FATHER FITZGERALD
I don't know what this is all about. Are you inferrin' somethin'?

CATHERINE
Only that there isn't a Father Giovanni at the rectory. And if ya truly were a priest at Sacred Hearts, you would know that, wouldn't ya?

THOMAS
Some other photos ya might be interested in. Remember, the school project I was workin' on? I took a series of rapid-fire shots of ya during the blessin' ceremony. I paid particular attention ta your arms as ya crossed yourself. Each of these photos has an exposure number on the back, tellin' me the order in which they were taken. *(He lays them out side by side.)* If I lay them

out side by side, in consecutive order, they tell a story... not unlike an animated short at the cinema. Look closely... I knew there was somethin' odd about what ya were doin'.

MARGUERITE

We all know, the proper way is to start at the head. *(She physically demonstrates.)* The Father, the Son, the Holy Spirit. But that's not what ya did at all.

THOMAS

Ya reversed it, didn't ya? Look at the photos. Everythin' is done backward. Ya created an inverted cross with your hands... a practice of Satan's worshippers.

EILEEN

And last night Marguerite was sleep-walkin' again. She began to channel the spirit of the little girl we think has been hauntin' our home, Agatha. She gave me a most tellin' clue from the spirit of Agatha herself...

MARGUERITE
Believe not the false facades,
Of witches and male witchers.-
Their truths shall be revealed to you,
Look close, their final pictures.

EILEEN

At first I thought she was referrin' to pictures of Jesse Purdy hangin' from the Sycamore. But she was talkin' about these photos of you. *You* wear the false façade. *You* are the Trojan horse.

THOMAS

And here's your book. The one on how to place proper curses upon a home. Ya clearly got it from the library and ya left it here by accident for us to find. Pretty careless, I would say, of someone who was so carefully tryin' ta destroy our family.

CATHERINE

The clincher however, was the note that John wrote just before he died. All this time we'd been misreadin' his chicken scratch. We thought it said "The colored man poisoned his host". But if ya look more closely, through candlelight, the writin' becomes more clear. John wrote "The *collared* man poisoned *the* host".

EILEEN

That's you. The 'collared' man is you. And 'the host', in this case, is the holy wafer.

CATHERINE

Jesse Purdy never hurt John. He was a sleepwalker like Marguerite, it's true. But he was a gentle soul. He must've come in after you'd left from givin' communion to John that night. We'd left the door unlocked, he just walked in, carryin' his equipment. All he did was give my husband a glass of water. You're the one poisoned him.

(A pause. The 'priest' says nothing but begins clapping his hands very slowly, then picks up the pace till it is loud and awkward. He then drops the Irish dialect altogether.)

FATHER FITZGERALD

Well done! Well done! What an extraordinary presentation. What a perceptive family of little detectives you are. That Mr. Doyle himself couldn't have written a better murder mystery. And you are right. I have been somewhat careless what with the book and all. But you've got to admit, the whole Catholic priest thing, with the collar and all? A stroke of genius, wasn't it?

CATHERINE
Who the Hell are ya?

FATHER FITZGERALD
My real name is Jeremiah Ketchum. I'm a direct descendant of John Ketchum. I understand you already know who he was. A witch who practiced his craft upon this land. His land. I'm here to protect what has been rightfully my family's for a very long time. You see, I followed in the 'family business', you might say. I've studied and practiced the dark arts for years. I awakened the dormant spirit of Agatha, John Ketcham's murdered daughter. Her unresolved anger is what possesses this house.

CATHERINE
How did you pull this off? Where were you stayin'?

FATHER FITZGERALD
I was never at the rectory, of course. I've been staying at the local youth hostel for the past few weeks.

CATHERINE
And that's how you had access to a telephone. That's the number you gave us reach you. But who did ya get to answer the phone?

FATHER FITZGERALD
I did most of the time. I've made myself indispensable there. I've had access to the front desk. How does this sound?... *(In his Irish dialect)* "Thank ya for callin' the Rectory of Sacred Hearts. Father Garrett Fitzgerald speakin'. How may I direct your call?" No one at the youth hostel ever caught on.

CATHERINE

How did ya know when ta answer the phone that way?

FATHER FITZGERALD

You'd be amazed how Satan can bestow the
gift of clairvoyance to his devotees.

CATHERINE

And the initial letter I mailed last month requesting a blessin'?

FATHER FITZGERALD

Oh, I intercepted that. This house was being watched.

CATHERINE

You were in Salem. How did you know we
were buildin' our house on this land?

FATHER FITZGERALD

I have operatives everywhere. Informants. They contacted me…. Details, details. What does it matter now?

CATHERINE

Ya had no cause ta kill John! Ya could've played
hocus pocus on this house without murder!

FATHER FITZGERALD

Your husband died because he needed to die. He was my biggest obstacle. The man of the house is always the greatest threat to witchcraft and evil curses. His corpse in your home helped to create a portal. The only way to positively create a true and pure channel for evil to invade a home is to commit murder. A dead body in the home provides a potent alchemy for the devil.

MARGUERITE
Da was growin' ill day by day. Ya gradually poisoned him, didn't ya? Bit by bit. So, ya could escape detection. How did ya do it? What did ya use?

FATHER FITZGERALD
Small traces of arsenic. From my hands to his. Every time I shook hands with him or slapped him on the back or embraced him, I was wearing my gloves. I was careful not to contaminate anyone else. Just him. It was only a matter of time until he scratched his lip or touched his mouth, delivering the poison to his system. The doses were small enough to make him sick but not kill him. The holy wafer, completely saturated with arsenic,… that was the coup de grace.

EILEEN
Well, at least now we know who you really are and why you cursed us.

THOMAS
Two innocent men are dead. And all for what?

MARGUERITE
You murdered our father. And Jesse Purdy hanged himself because of what you did.

FATHER FITZGERALD
Collateral damage.

EILEEN
You're a cruel and evil man.

FATHER FITZGERALD
Now, now,…. Flattery will get you everywhere.

EILEEN
Ya make me ill.

THOMAS
You're a sick twist.

FATHER FITZGERALD
I have to tell you, you do take a good picture, Thomas. Seeing these photographs of that dead man bleeding from the noose cutting into his throat,… his stiff, lifeless body hanging there like a prize hog,… His eyes bulging, and the ashen pallor of his skin,… It does my heart good. Just another insignificant life sacrificed for the greater glory of the Prince of Darkness.

CATHERINE
Get out! Get out of our house!

FATHER FITZGERALD
All right. I'll leave. My work here is done… Move out. Tear the house down. Leave our land alone. Let Agatha Ketchum lie here in peace on the grounds where she's buried.

THOMAS
You're guilty of murder. The law will find ya and try ya.

FATHER FITZGERALD
You'd need my confession. And you'll never get it.

CATHERINE
Our home is completely possessed by evil spirits.
What are we supposed to do now?

FATHER FITZGERALD
Move out. Tear the house down. Leave our land alone.

CATHERINE
Never.

FATHER FITZGERALD
Never?

CATHERINE
I'll protect this house to the end in Jesus' name!

FATHER FITZGERALD
In Jesus' name?!!!
JESUS CHRIST IS DEAD!!! WHO WILL SAVE YOU NOW?!

EILEEN
You'll never get away with this.

FATHER FITZGERALD
I already have!

THOMAS
Get out now while ya still can!

MARGUERITE
The Lord will have vengeance on ya!

THOMAS
I'll rip ya apart now, ya Bastard!

(The 'priest' takes a position of power center with his arms spread wide and appears to beckon all the powers of darkness. The house explodes in a flurry of paranormal activity.)

FATHER FITZGERALD
Maledico tibi omnes duplices! Contabescant in Inferno! So mote it be!

(In the growing chaos, the family explodes in anger. The following five lines are yelled out simultaneously. On top of one another…)

CATHERINE
Get the out of our house!
Come Hell or high water,
We'll defeat the evils manifest here!

EILEEN
You're just duplicitous swine!
Murderer! Murderer! May we
see ya rot in Hell fires! Leave
us now!

FATHER FITZGERALD
It's not too late to reject that
Nazarene! Join me and Lucifer
himself in the conflagration
of eternal flames!

MARGUERITE
We rebuke your evil. Ya killed my
dear Da and you'll be payin'
for it now! If not now, the
after life!

THOMAS
I'll kill ya, I will! Give me
Half a chance and I'll
Get vengeance for Da's murder!

(At this moment, Jeremiah Ketchum grabs John Moynahan's scythe and raises it high to bring down upon the heads of the Moynahan family.)

FATHER FITZGERALD
MEET YOUR NEW FATHER!!!!

(Jesse Purdy, looking dead, ashen, like a zombie, blood streaming from his neck, bursts through the front door. He carries a noose in his hand. The 'priest' screams as do all the rest in the home. Jeremiah drops the scythe immediately. It appears that Purdy has come back from the dead seeking vengeance. Everyone runs for cover with the exception of the 'priest' who is rooted to the spot at center of the living room. He is crouched upon the floor, cowering in fear as Purdy approaches him.)

JESSE
WHERE'S THE BEAST WHO KILLED THE HOST?!
(He sees Ketcham and advances toward him.)

FATHER FITZGERALD
NOOO!!! You're dead! You killed yourself! Help me!

JESSE
WHAT DID YOU DO?!

FATHER FITZGERALD
I did it, I did it! I killed your friend! I put a curse on this house! Please! Go back to the Hell from whence you came! You undead thing! Please! Someone save me!

(Jesse brings the hand-held sickle to Ketcham's neck and it appears he is preparing to cut his throat.)

FATHER FITZGERALD
NOOOOOO!!!!!!!!!

(A pause, then suddenly, Jesse tosses the sickle on the floor. He sits on a chair. A pause.)

JESSE
I always wanted to be an actor.

(The family rises from their cowering positions. They relax.)

JESSE
How was that?

EILEEN
Ya nearly had me convinced.

THOMAS
I love the part when ya pulled out the sickle.

EILEEN
My favorite was callin' him a beast.

MARGUERITE
I think the make-up was the best.

FATHER FITZGERALD
What the Hell is going on? What have you all done?

CATHERINE
Just a little play-actin' for your benefit. Don't ya think we pulled it off rather well, Mr. Ketcham?

FATHER FITZGERALD
But the pictures! I saw your body hanging from a tree!

THOMAS
Illusion. We staged the whole thing. I cropped out the best part.

EILEEN
If you'd seen the lower half, you'd have seen Mr. Purdy standing on a pickle barrel.

JESSE
Amazing what a little cock's blood can do.

CATHERINE
Here, I'll help ya wipe that off.

JESSE
Thank you, Mrs. Moynahan.

FATHER FITZGERALD
You were in on this.

JESSE
I never committed suicide. After a lot of soul searching, I knew I couldn't have been the one to kill the Host. We got together this morning, gathered our evidence, and made our plan. This part was my idea. I said tell that

bastard I hung myself. Show him 'proof'. Let him believe it. If the family can't get him to confess, then my bloody corpse will.

MARGUERITE
Thank you, Mr Purdy.

JESSE
You're most welcome.

CATHERINE
I almost told ya to forget it. He had what we needed. He'd already admitted to us that he'd murdered John by arsenic. But your little performance just confirmed his guilt.

(Marguerite goes to the telephone.)

JESSE
Glad I could be of service.

CATHERINE
And now you've officially confessed to the police.

FATHER FITZGERALD
The police? What police?

(Marguerite puts the receiver to her ear.)

MARGUERITE
Did ya get all that, Chief Quinn? Yes, Jeremiah Ketcham. Yes, he's turnin' himself in. Mr. Purdy will be escortin' him there. Thank ya, Chief Quinn. *(Marguerite hangs up the telephone receiver. She speaks to Ketcham.)* We figured Chief Quinn at the police department would love to hear anythin'

and everythin' ya had ta say to us. So, I called the precinct just before you arrived. I never hung up the receiver. I just kept it right here on the table. He heard it all… Word for word.

(Jesse pulls Ketcham to his feet.)

FATHER FITZGERALD
Sorry, Eileen. What can I say? We had some laughs… Right?

JESSE
Let's go.

(Just as Jesse muscles Ketcham to the front door, Ketcham stops defiantly and addresses the family. Jesse lets him get his final words in.)

FATHER FITZGERALD
There's no cure for what this house has now.
Not enough holy water in the world.

(Music in. Jesse leads Ketcham out through the front door. Exit. Only the surviving four family members are left. Lights fade. Catherine goes out the front door, watches stage left as if to see Jesse leading Ketcham away. She sits on the top step. A warm glow rises on her. She speaks to the audience.)

CATHERINE
And with that, the seed of evil was excised, though
the blight would continue to fester.

[End of Scene]

Scene 6

"We Are Resolved"

(Lights fade to a mellow sepia. Gentle music eases in. Catherine and children go out to the steps leading up to the front door. Late afternoon shadows of skeletal trees and Autumnal foliage appear across the outer stoop. John's ghost enters. Catherine sits and motions with her hands for her children to come closer to her. They do. All sit on the steps and create a lovely tableau. In more ominous, yet oddly hopeful music, John's ghost enters, strolls about the living room, then lifts his arms toward the old grandfather's clock. Suddenly, in fog and blue light emanating, the little ghost girl of Agatha Ketcham, in all white, slowly enters from the clock, trance-like. She walks up to John. She takes his hands. He leads her off stage left into the eternal peace of Elysium. Music fades.)

CATHERINE
Spirits abound in this new land -
Breathin', longin', reachin'

EILEEN
With outstretched tendrils,
As woodland branches –

MARGUERITE
Summonin' us into their mysterious lair,
Enfoldin' us into their pagan universe.

THOMAS
We are here now,
Within the within –

~ AMITYVILLE 1925 ~

EILEEN
A house that is not quite ours –

MARGUERITE
Yet here we'll live –

THOMAS
Yet here we'll die –

CATHERINE
And haunt this home in contented perpetuity.

(At this point the ghost of John Moynahan has joined his living family, unbeknownst to them. In a sweet and soft rendering, all five stare off into the distance and sing the final verses of "The Wind that Shakes the Barley", acapella.)

CATHERINE
"But blood for blood
Without remorse I've
Taken at Oulart Hollow

ALL
And laid my true love's
Clay-cold corpse where
I full soon may follow

And 'round his grave
I wander drear, noon,
Night and early mornin'

With breakin' heart
When e'er I hear the wind

That shakes the barley

With breaking heart
When e'er I hear the wind
That shakes the barley
…the barley
…the barley"

(Fade to Black)

[End of Play]

The Playwright

Christofer Cook holds a Master of Fine Arts in Directing for the Stage from the Theatre Conservatory of Roosevelt University in Chicago, Illinois. He has also earned a Master of Arts in Professional Counseling from South University, as well as a Bachelor of Arts in Drama from Winthrop College. His most recent plays are *An Edgar Allan Poe Christmas Carol* and *Amityville 1925*. Other published plays include *Dracula of Transylvania*, *Phantom of the Opera*, *The Legend of Sleepy Hollow*, and *A Christmas Carolinian*. He is a member of the Horror Writer's Association and the Dramatists Guild of America. Mr. Cook is a native of Columbia, South Carolina.

Printed in Great Britain
by Amazon